"I am happy," Roberta thought. "I have never been so happy."

She knew her happiness was centered on the man who was trying to portray her on canvas.

"You have been very good," Adam said, rising from his stool and walking towards her. "Now I feel it is a waste of time to be painting when I might be kissing you."

"How . . . far have you . . . got with my portrait?" Roberta asked and knew her voice trembled.

"Not far enough," he replied. "Just as it is impossible to capture the sunlight, so I cannot capture your beauty."

He kissed her fingers one by one, then turned her hand over to kiss her palm, a long, lingering kiss which made her quiver . . .

LOVE COMES WEST

A Camfield Novel of Love

Camfield Place,
Hatfield
Hertfordshire,
England

Dearest Reader,

This starts a new and very exciting era of my books with Jove. They already have nearly two hundred of my books which they have had ever since they became the first publisher to bring out my books in America. Now all my paperbacks in future will be published by them.

As you already know, Camfield Place in Hertfordshire is my home, which originally existed in 1275, but was rebuilt in 1867 by the grandfather of Beatrix Potter.

It was here in this lovely house, with the best view of the county, that she wrote *The Tale of Peter Rabbit*. Mr. McGregor's garden is exactly as she described it. The door in the wall that the fat little rabbit could not squeeze underneath and the goldfish pool where the white cat sat twitching its tail are still there.

I had Camfield Place blessed when I came here in 1950 and was so happy with my husband until he died, and now with my children and grandchildren, that I know the atmosphere is filled with love and we have all been very lucky.

It is easy here to write of love and I feel you will enjoy the new Camfield Novels of Love, which are a little different from those that you have read before. The plots are definitely more exciting and the covers more romantic. They come to you, like all my novels, with love.

Bless you,

Books by Barbara Cartland

THE ADVENTURER
AGAIN THIS RAPTURE
ARMOUR AGAINST LOVE
THE AUDACIOUS ADVENTURESS
BARBARA CARTLAND'S BOOK OF BEAUTY AND HEALTH
THE BITTER WINDS OF LOVE
BLUE HEATHER
BROKEN BARRIERS
THE CAPTIVE HEART
THE COIN OF LOVE
THE COMPLACENT WIFE
COUNT THE STARS
CUPID RIDES PILLION
DANCE ON MY HEART
DESIRE OF THE HEART
DESPERATE DEFIANCE
THE DREAM WITHIN
A DUEL OF HEARTS
ELIZABETH EMPRESS OF AUSTRIA
ELIZABETHAN LOVER
THE ENCHANTED MOMENT
THE ENCHANTED WALTZ
THE ENCHANTING EVIL
ESCAPE FROM PASSION
FOR ALL ETERNITY
A GHOST IN MONTE CARLO
THE GOLDEN GONDOLA
A HALO FOR THE DEVIL
A HAZARD OF HEARTS
A HEART IS BROKEN
THE HEART OF THE CLAN
THE HIDDEN EVIL
THE HIDDEN HEART
THE HORIZONS OF LOVE
AN INNOCENT IN MAYFAIR

IN THE ARMS OF LOVE
THE IRRESISTIBLE BUCK
JOSEPHINE EMPRESS OF FRANCE
THE KISS OF PARIS
THE KISS OF THE DEVIL
A KISS OF SILK
THE KNAVE OF HEARTS
THE LEAPING FLAME
A LIGHT TO THE HEART
LIGHTS OF LOVE
THE LITTLE PRETENDER
LOST ENCHANTMENT
LOST LOVE
LOVE AND LINDA
LOVE AT FORTY
LOVE FORBIDDEN
LOVE HOLDS THE CARDS
LOVE IN HIDING
LOVE IN PITY
LOVE IS AN EAGLE
LOVE IS CONTRABAND
LOVE IS DANGEROUS
LOVE IS MINE
LOVE IS THE ENEMY
LOVE ME FOREVER
LOVE ON THE RUN
LOVE TO THE RESCUE
LOVE UNDER FIRE
THE MAGIC OF HONEY
MESSENGER OF LOVE
METTERNICH: THE PASSIONATE DIPLOMAT
MONEY, MAGIC AND MARRIAGE
NO HEART IS FREE
THE ODIOUS DUKE
OPEN WINGS
OUT OF REACH
THE PASSIONATE PILGRIM
THE PRETTY HORSEBREAKERS
THE PRICE IS LOVE

A RAINBOW TO HEAVEN
THE RELUCTANT BRIDE
THE RUNAWAY HEART
THE SCANDALOUS LIFE OF KING CAROL
THE SECRET FEAR
THE SMUGGLED HEART
A SONG OF LOVE
STARS IN MY HEART
STOLEN HALO
SWEET ADVENTURE
SWEET ENCHANTRESS
SWEET PUNISHMENT
THEFT OF A HEART
THE THIEF OF LOVE
THIS TIME IT'S LOVE
TOUCH A STAR
TOWARDS THE STARS
THE UNKNOWN HEART
THE UNPREDICTABLE BRIDE
A VIRGIN IN PARIS
WE DANCED ALL NIGHT
WHERE IS LOVE?
THE WINGS OF ECSTASY
THE WINGS OF LOVE
WINGS ON MY HEART
WOMAN—THE ENIGMA

CAMFIELD NOVELS OF LOVE

THE POOR GOVERNESS
WINGED VICTORY
LUCKY IN LOVE
LOVE AND THE MARQUIS
A MIRACLE IN MUSIC
LIGHT OF THE GODS
BRIDE TO A BRIGAND
LOVE COMES WEST

A NEW CAMFIELD NOVEL OF LOVE BY

BARBARA CARTLAND

Love Comes West

A JOVE BOOK

LOVE COMES WEST

A Jove Book / published by arrangement with
the author

PRINTING HISTORY
Jove edition / April 1984

ISBN: 0-515-07607-4

Jove books are published by The Berkley Publishing Group, Inc.
200 Madison Avenue, New York, N.Y. 10016.
The words "A JOVE BOOK" and the "J" with sunburst
are trademarks belonging to Jove Publications, Inc.

PRINTED IN THE UNITED STATES OF AMERICA

Author's Note

When I visited San Francisco in 1983 for the first time I was astonished and intrigued by this fantastic and unique City.

I found its up and downhill roads, its delicious restaurants, its harbour and the streets of Chinatown all fascinating.

Where else in this day and age can one look out of a restaurant window on the Quay when eating oysters and see a collection of sea lions in the bay?

Where else can one eat excellent French cuisine in a restaurant described as resembling a Brothel?

San Francisco is unusual, fantastic and always exciting!

chapter one

1885

THE Earl of Wentworth was dying.

The heat in the tent, even though it was black like a Bedouin one, was intolerable, and although the side was open there was not a breath of wind to stir the leaves of the palm trees in the oasis.

Roberta dipped a piece of cloth into the water, which having been poured from a goat's-skin was almost as warm as the air, and wiped his forehead.

He had been either asleep or unconscious for a long time, but now he opened his eyes.

"Would you like a drink, Papa?" she asked.

For a moment it seemed as if her father could not understand, then he nodded very slightly.

She fetched the drink she had already prepared of brandy and water which was standing in a bowl to keep it cool.

Gently she lifted his head and held the rim to his lips.

Although the Earl's face was very pale from his illness,

he was still a handsome and very attractive man and it was understandable, Roberta thought involuntarily, that many women loved him.

He took a few sips of the brandy and it seemed to revive him slightly, for as she laid his head gently back against the pillow he said:

"I am—sorry—dearest."

"For what, Papa? You cannot help being ill."

"I am dying—as you well—know," the Earl replied, "and in a very—inconvenient—place."

Roberta gave a little cry.

"Do not talk like that, Papa! You know I cannot lose you. What would I do without you?"

The Earl took a deep breath as if to give himself strength. Then he said:

"Listen—my precious, because we have very—little time. When I am dead—bury me—here in the—sand."

Roberta would have protested, but she realized what an effort her father was having to make to talk to her and thought it best to keep silent.

"Hassam will take you—safely to—Algiers," her father went on as if he was following his own thoughts. "Tell the men you cannot—pay them until you get—there. That will ensure you have no—trouble."

"I will do that," Roberta murmured.

Again there was silence. Her father had closed his eyes and she thought he had finished, but after a moment he said:

"I have been—thinking of how—uncomfortable it will be for you to—go home."

"I know, Papa," Roberta agreed, "and that is why you cannot die and leave me alone. You know how disagreeable the family will be to me when I return."

The Earl nodded his head as if he understood and after a moment he said:

"Go to your—Aunt Margaret—she is the best of my sisters—and I think you would be—happy with—her."

Roberta looked puzzled.

"You must—remember," the Earl said as if she had questioned him, "that your Aunt Margaret was more like—me than the rest of my relatives and ran away with an—American Preacher."

"Yes, of course!" Roberta exclaimed. "I remember it now."

"Her name is Dulaine—and you will find a—letter from her written—I must admit—nearly two years ago—amongst my papers in the—Bank in Algiers."

"America is a long way off, Papa!" Roberta murmured.

"I know," her father agreed. "At the same time—you have the choice between being—punished by the family for my sins—or else making a new life for yourself—in a new world with—your Aunt Margaret."

His pale lips twisted in a faint smile as he said:

"I know which I would—choose."

With an effort Roberta managed to say:

"It will be an adventure, Papa, but not the same if you are not sharing it with me."

"I wish I could—go with you," the Earl replied. "I would—like to see—America."

He shut his eyes again, and Roberta realised that the effort he had made to talk to her had been superhuman.

Once again she held the glass of brandy to his lips, but although he obediently took two small sips of it she felt as if he was drifting away from her.

Sitting back on her heels beside the bed, which was nothing more than a mattress on the sandy floor, Roberta wondered frantically if there was anything she could do.

She knew her father was right when he said he was dying. The same fever had killed his mistress a month earlier, and her body now lay buried outside a small Arab village without even a cross to mark the place.

"Why could I have not died too?" Roberta asked.

The fever which had swept through the caravan had caused the deaths of two camel-boys and of Francine, with whom her father had been deeply infatuated.

He had succumbed to the same fever which had left him limp, bloodless, and with no strength to go on living.

Looking back, Roberta thought it was almost a miracle that they had survived so long without any illnesses, or indeed any other setbacks, in their strange, fascinating wanderings in North Africa.

It was something she had never expected to happen to her when, having inherited her father's spirit of independence and sense of adventure, she had found the courage to run away from the gaunt, dark house in Essex.

It was there that her relatives never stopped finding fault and telling her what a disgrace her father was to the family.

Because she had found their restrictions and eternal criticims intolerable she could understand how her father, after her mother's death, had found England unendurable.

Without any warning he had therefore left Worth Park, his ancestral home, one morning never to return.

The fact that he had taken with him the wife of the Lord Lieutenant of the County did not make his behaviour any more excusable in the eyes of those whom he had left behind.

Roberta's grandmother, the Dowager Countess, had arrived with Lady Emily, her youngest and unmarried daughter, to close up the Park before taking Roberta to live with them in Essex.

4

She could remember resenting at the time that, having lost her mother two years earlier, she must now lose her father, the horses she loved, and the old servants who had looked after her since she was a child.

What was more, her grandmother dispensed with the services of her Governess on the ground that she was frivolous.

She arranged instead for Lady Emily to give Roberta some lessons, while an elderly retired teacher was brought daily from the neighbouring village to instruct her in the subjects in which her aunt could not profess to be proficient.

Because Roberta was very intelligent, she found the lessons as dull as the life she was now expected to lead with two elderly women whose closest bond in common was that they violently disapproved of her father.

Every day she was forced to listen to long tirades about his disgraceful behaviour, and any effort she made at being charming, looking pretty, or even laughing merely brought the rebuke that it reminded them of 'poor, misguided Duncan.'

Had Roberta been younger she might perhaps have begun to believe that her father was as immoral and wicked as they made him out to be.

But she was nearly fourteen when he left and she could remember all too vividly how handsome and charming he was, and how the tempo always seemed to rise when he came into a room.

She could recall, too, how every woman, however old she might be, had a flirtatious expression in her eyes when she looked at him.

There was the memory also of how happy they had all been when her mother was alive.

There had been house-parties every weekend, people continually spending the day or a few nights with them, hunting and shooting in the winter, boating on the lake and picnics in the woods in the summer.

Everything they had done seemed to have evoked peals of happy laughter.

Only Roberta had known how miserable her father had been when her mother died and the sunlight had seemed to have left the house.

It was then he had started going to London in an effort to forget, and he always came back looking better and with amusing stories to tell Roberta of the Theatres he had visited, the supper-parties he had enjoyed, and the people he had met.

She had the idea later that these seldom included the social personalities who had so often stayed with them at home.

Instead he told her of the attractiveness of the Gaiety Girls, the amusing Artists who appeared at the Music Halls, and the gay nights that he had spent at Romano's and other notorious restaurants where she knew she would never be allowed to dine or sup.

Then after her father's absences in London had grown more and more frequent, suddenly everything changed.

He now appeared to prefer the country where he would ride with the attractive Lady Bingham who was married to the Lord Lieutenant.

She was his second wife, very much younger than her husband, and Roberta thought how lovely she was and that she would like to look like her when she grew up.

Sometimes her father and Lady Bingham would take her riding with them, and occasionally she joined them on the river or for luncheon.

In the summer when it was hot, the Earl ordered the meals to be served out of doors in the Grecian Temple at the end of the garden.

It seemed to Roberta that it was almost as if her mother was back, because her father laughed and everything she and Lady Bingham said appeared to amuse him.

There was a new atmosphere of happiness, which she had never forgotten.

Then without the slightest warning her father had gone.

When he said good-night to her the night before he left, he had held her very close to him and there had been a serious note in his voice as he said:

"You are growing up, my darling, and you are going to be very pretty, or perhaps 'lovely' is the right word. I must think about your future and make sure you are chaperoned by somebody who can introduce you to society, so that you meet the right type of man who will make you a suitable husband."

Roberta had laughed.

"There is plenty of time for that, Papa, and I would much rather talk to you, dance with you, and just be with you than with any other man I have ever seen!"

Her father's arms had tightened around her as he had said:

"Thank you, my dearest one. That is a compliment I appreciate. At the same time my sort of life is not the best where you are concerned."

Roberta did not understand what he meant, and anyway she was very sleepy.

They had spent a wonderful day alone together and, although she was very fond of Lady Bingham who made everything so amusing, it was fun to have her father all to herself.

They had ridden away from the house soon after breakfast and gone all over the estate, almost as if her father was inspecting it.

For luncheon they had eaten bread and cheese and drunk

cider at an Inn several miles away from the house, riding home late in the afternoon.

Then they had spent a long time in the stables looking at the horses, and it was only afterwards that Roberta knew her father had been bidding them goodbye.

Then, the greatest joy of all, she had dined alone with him in the Dining-Room dressed in her best and prettiest gown.

He had talked to her as if she was grown up and she had even had a small glass of champagne.

After she was in bed he had come in to her room to kiss her good-night and said:

"Take good care of yourself, my adorable little daughter, and always remember that I love you."

"I love you too, Papa!" Roberta replied. "You are the most wonderful father any girl ever had!"

She felt the Earl drew in his breath before he bent down to kiss her forehead.

Then without saying any more he had left her bedroom, and she had fallen asleep.

In the morning she found he had left her a short note.

It said very little except that he had gone away to France and that he had asked his mother to close Worth Park and take her to live with her in Essex.

For a moment Roberta could hardly believe that her father meant to leave for ever.

Then when she realised that he had taken Lady Bingham with him she knew the scandal it would cause would make it impossible for him to return for a very long time.

What was more, the Lord Lieutenant was refusing to divorce his wife, which meant that if she and the Earl ever returned to England they would be completely ostracised.

And as the Dowager Countess never ceased to say: 'would never be accepted at Court!'

"How dare your father do anything so disgraceful?" was a question which Roberta was to hear repeated over and over again.

"A man in his position should have known better!"

"He has dragged our name into the dirt."

"He should be heartily ashamed of himself!"

She felt sometimes as if the same scathing remarks were being repeated and repeated so that even when she was alone they seemed to echo inside her head.

It was two years later that she learned not from her grandmother, but from what the servants were whispering amongst themselves, that Lady Bingham had returned home and her husband had forgiven her.

Of course a great number of people in the County would refuse to speak to her and as the Dowager Countess had predicted, she would never again be accepted at Court.

One day, Roberta was about to enter the Drawing-Room when she overheard her aunt say to a caller:

"No gentleman could have behaved more magnanimously to one who is nothing more than a scarlet woman!"

Arrested by the words, she had listened at the door, making no move to enter the room.

"And what had happened to your brother?" she heard the caller ask. "I have always thought him the most handsome man I have ever seen!"

"I am afraid Duncan's looks have been his undoing," Lady Emily had said sourly, "and doubtless he will console himself with somebody else."

"You do not think he will come home?"

"I imagine that would be very unlikely."

There was silence for a moment. Then the caller enquired:

"Where is he at the moment?"

"He was in Spain," Lady Emily replied, "but I heard

quite by chance from one of our cousins that he has rented a house in Paris for the Spring. I suppose he finds the gaiety of the French Capital very much to his taste!"

There was that sarcastic note in her aunt's voice with which Roberta was very familiar.

She was sure now that the denunciation of her father which had died down a little, would rise up all over again.

Quite suddenly she felt she could not bear it.

How could she spend the next two years, before she was expected to marry, listening to the tirades against which she had no defence?

She did not go into the Drawing-Room as she had intended.

Instead she went upstairs to her bedroom to sit at the window looking out.

She did not see the first green buds of Spring sprouting on the trees, the golden daffodils flowering in the long grass or the first baby lambs frisking in the fields.

Instead she saw her father's laughing face, his eyes twinkling, the magic of him making her feel as if everything was wildly exciting and that if she wanted she could jump over the moon.

"He is alone," she told herself, "and now I can go to him."

At sixteen she had developed what her teacher from the village described somewhat disparagingly as 'an intelligence beyond her years; something not particularly desirable in a young woman!'

Carefully Roberta made her plans.

She knew it would be impossible for her to travel to Paris alone, but she remembered that her grandmother had given a cottage on her estate in Essex to an elderly housemaid, now retired, who had accompanied her as a lady's-maid when she had had to move from Worth Park.

She had however not been happy at being uprooted from the estate where she had lived all her life, and where all her friends either lived in the village or else were working, as she had, in the 'Big House.'

She had hoped, when she had asked if she might retire, that she would be sent back to Worth Park, but the Dowager Countess had no wish to have anything to do with her son's estate which was now being managed by Solicitors.

Instead she had given Gracie, as the old woman was called, a cottage in the village.

It was impossible for her to refuse but Roberta was aware of how unhappy she was.

Because Gracie was almost her last contact with her home, she regularly visited her at least once a week, and they would talk about the old days when her mother was alive.

As Gracie admired her father and nothing would make her say a word against him, it was a joy to Roberta to hear him praised rather than abused.

It was therefore to Gracie she went the next morning, riding with a groom and leaving him to hold her horse when she went inside the small cottage.

"Oh, it's you, M'Lady!" Gracie exclaimed when Roberta appeared. "I was hoping to see you. I've got something to tell you!"

"I know what it is, Gracie," Roberta answered. "You have heard that Lady Bingham has returned home."

"Oh, you knows already!" Gracie exclaimed, obviously disappointed at not being first with the news.

"Yes, I have already heard," Roberta admitted, "and now that Papa is alone, I intend to join him."

"You're never going to do that!" Gracie exclaimed in

astonishment. "What'll your grandmother say?"

"She will say a great deal," Roberta replied, "but only after I have gone!"

"D'you mean you're leaving without telling her?"

"I will keep them guessing as to where I am," Roberta smiled. "Actually I am going to Paris to find Papa, and you are coming with me!"

Gracie, who was very energetic and spry at sixty-nine, looked at her in astonishment.

"Did you say—*I* were a–coming with you, M'Lady?"

"Yes, Gracie. You know quite well I cannot travel alone. Mama would not have approved, and therefore you have to look after me."

Gracie gasped in astonishment, but because she loved Roberta and was actually thrilled at the idea of going away she agreed to everything that was suggested.

It was not easy, but once Roberta had made up her mind she could be as determined as her father when the occasion arose, and everything seemed to fall into place.

She had no ready money because she seldom went shopping and her grandmother gave her only the same amount of pocket-money she had received when she lived with her father and mother.

This was actually not enough to get her to Paris, so she planned to wait until the end of the month when the servants in the house, as well as those employed on the estate, would be paid.

This meant that the Estate Manager, a slow-thinking, middle-aged man, would come to the Hall the afternoon before and sit in the room which was known as 'The Estate Office,' and count out all the money which would be given out the following morning.

When he had put it into neat little bags he would lock them up in the safe for the night and hand the keys to the

Countess, leaving everything in what he called 'apple-pie order.'

That afternoon Roberta waited until she had heard him say goodbye to her grandmother, when as usual the Countess placed the keys in the righthand drawer of her desk before going upstairs to change for dinner.

It took Roberta very little time to collect them, go to the safe, open it, empty all the little bags of money into a small case she had ready, and leave a piece of paper on which she had written:

> *I owe you the money I have taken from here and which will be repaid by my father, the Earl of Wentworth.*

She had signed it with a flourish, placed it in a prominent position, and put the keys back in the desk.

Then she had gone demurely upstairs to say good-night to her grandmother and her Aunt Emily before she ate her supper alone in the School-Room.

Because she was only sixteen, it was only on special occasions that she was allowed to dine downstairs.

However, as she found dinner in the Dining-Room, waited on by a Butler and two footmen, long-drawn-out and extremely boring, she much preferred to eat alone and read a book at the same time.

But that night she was too excited to read, and having sent away most of the well-cooked, nourishing, but dull dishes that were brought to her, she went to her bedroom to make sure that everything was ready for the morning.

The most awkward problem had been how to get the local brougham which was for hire to call at the house without her grandmother being aware of it.

Then Gracie had come to her aid.

"If I says one of my relatives be ill, M'Lady, I can hire Tom Hanson to take me to the station, and he'll call for me at whatever time I tells him to."

"Of course, Gracie! I might have thought of that myself!" Roberta exclaimed. "Will you tell him to be outside your house at four-thirty in the morning, so that we can catch the milk-train to London which I know leaves from Chelmsford at five o'clock."

"I'll do that, M'Lady," Gracie agreed.

It was therefore as dawn was rising over the trees in the Park that Roberta reached the stables.

All she was taking with her was a small carpet-bag that contained only necessities and two of her lightest dresses.

They had been chosen for her by her grandmother, and she was quite certain her father would think them as un-attractive as she did and buy her something new.

The same applied to the very plain gown in which she was to travel and the coat that went over it.

It was her Sunday best, and every time she put it on she felt as if she might have come out of an Orphanage.

Her bonnet was the same dark blue as the rest of her outfit, and was trimmed with the blue ribbons which seemed to have no colour in them.

It presented no difficulty to Roberta to saddle one of the horses she habitually rode and to ride it holding her carpet-bag on the saddle in front of her.

When she reached Gracie's cottage she saw with a leap of her heart that Tom Hanson's brougham was outside and that he was just walking up the small path to knock on the cottage door.

There was a light in the window which told her that Gracie was ready.

As she dismounted with some difficulty because she was

still holding her bag in her hand Tom Hanson turned around to stare at her in astonishment.

"'Morning, M'Lady!" he said. "An' where might ye be a–goin'?"

"I am coming with you, Tom," Roberta replied. "It is a long journey for Gracie to make on her own, so I have decided to accompany her."

"That's right kind o' Your Ladyship," Tom exclaimed, "but what are ye going to do wi' yer 'orse?"

"I shall turn him loose on the village green," Roberta replied. "He will not go far, and I thought you might be kind enough when you return from the station to take him back to the Hall for me."

Tom Hanson scratched his head.

"Oi'll do that right enough, M'Lady," he said, "but what's 'appened to all them grooms in th' stables?"

"They were asleep," Roberta said lightly, "and it was quicker for me to come alone than to wake one of them up."

Tom laughed and she was certain this was a joke would be repeated against the grooms for a long time to come.

Then she and Gracie were off and she knew that it would be at least four or five hours before anybody realised she had gone. By then it would be too late to stop her, even if they guessed where she was going.

She had left a note for her grandmother, but was too wise to say she had gone to her father, thinking perhaps they would telegraph to the authorities to stop her at Dover.

Instead she wrote that she had suddenly heard that a dear friend was ill and had gone by train to visit her, taking Gracie with her as she was certain her grandmother would not like her to travel alone.

This made it sound so correct that she knew it would

never enter her grandmother's head for one moment that she was doing anything so reprehensible as to travel to Paris.

Thinking back on it afterwards, Roberta was astonished that everything went so smoothly.

They managed to catch the morning train to Dover which connected with the afternoon cross-Channel Steamer.

She could afford, with the money she had taken from the safe, to travel in every comfort, and it was therefore not an arduous journey, except that they did not reach Paris until early the next morning.

It was then Roberta encountered the real difficulty, which was to find her father.

Afterwards he scolded her for embarking on such an escapade without knowing exactly where she could find him.

"I remembered two things, Papa," Roberta explained blithely. "First, that when you took Mama to Paris I wrote to you care of the Travellers' Club, and secondly, you told me that your English Bank was situated in Paris in the *Rue de la Paix*."

The Earl looked at her in astonishment.

"Whatever made you remember that?"

"I suppose because the way you and Mama talked about the *Rue de la Paix* made it sound to me the most exciting street in the whole world!"

"That is what it was to your mother?" the Earl laughed. "Mr. Worth works there, and no woman who came to Paris could resist buying one of his creations the moment she arrived!"

That was true, Roberta thought, because the gowns her mother had bought at Worth's were the most beautiful she had ever seen.

Anyway, knowing she must wait until the Bank opened,

Roberta had taken Gracie, who by this time was too bemused to ask any questions, to an Hotel next to the station.

When they had eaten a large breakfast they had sat in the comfortable Lounge until it was after eight o'clock.

Then when Gracie's head was nodding with fatigue despite the fact that she had slept most of the way in the train, though Roberta felt as bright as the birds which by now would be singing in the gardens of England, they had driven to the Bank in the *Rue de la Paix*.

When she had explained to the Manager who she was, he had given her her father's address without too much prevarication.

It was nine-thirty when the *voiture* which Roberta had hired drew up outside a tall, rather distinguished looking house in a quiet street just off the Champs Elysées.

The Earl was having breakfast when the French servant, making no effort to announce her, opened the door and let her into the Dining-Room.

For a moment her father could only stare at her in astonishment as if he did not believe she was real.

Then as Roberta ran towards him he rose to his feet exclaiming in astonishment:

"My precious, is it really you?"

"Yes, it is me, Papa! Do you not recognise me?" Roberta asked feeling, although she was smiling, curiously like tears now that her journey was at an end.

She flung her arms around her father, and as he held her close against him and she kissed his cheek the Earl asked:

"Why are you here? What has happened? Why did you not let me know that you were coming?"

"I have run away, just as you did, Papa!" Roberta replied breathlessly. "I heard you were alone and I could not stand Grandmama's and Aunt Emily's croakings any longer! Since

17

Lady Bingham has returned to her husband, they have started to say how wicked you are all over again, and I refuse to put up with it any longer!"

The Earl hugged her.

"My darling, this is madness! Delicious madness! God, I am pleased to see you! I cannot tell you how much I have missed you!"

"As I have missed you, Papa."

Now, to her surprise, tears were rolling down her cheeks and she was kissing him, kissing him over and over again as if she could hardly believe he was really there.

Then it seemed as if neither of them could ever stop talking; there was so much to say, so much to ask, so much to remember.

It was typical of the Earl, that because it was what Roberta wanted, he accepted what she had done, and never suggested that she should return.

"You realise, my dearest, that if you stay with me, it will not be possible for you to be a conventional débutante? I am sure you would never be allowed to make your curtsey at Buckingham Palace."

"All that matters is that I should be with you, Papa," Roberta replied. "If I stay any longer with Grandmama I shall die of boredom, or else become a terrible bore myself. Then no man will look at me, let alone wish to marry me!"

"The first thing you can do," the Earl said disparagingly, "is to throw away those clothes! They would make even Aphrodite look plain, and that is an understatement!"

It was not only what he said, but the way he said it, and suddenly Roberta was laughing helplessly and he was laughing too.

It was like stepping into Paradise after being incarcerated in the darkest Hades that had ever imprisoned Persephone.

As might have been expected, the Earl did not alter his way of life because his daughter was living with him.

There were beautiful women to amuse him in the evenings, and occasionally he took Roberta out to luncheon with them or they rode all together in the Park.

During most of the time they were in Paris, he spent part of the day with his daughter and left her alone in the evening.

He insisted that she have a Tutor to teach her French, and a dancing-master as well as a music-master to call at the house and give her lessons.

While he was amusing himself in his own way he arranged that Roberta should attend the Opera and the Theatres wherever there were Plays which he considered suitable for her to see.

Her French teacher took her round the Museums and Art Galleries and they visited Versailles, Fontainebleau, and of course, Notre Dame.

It was all so different from studying the subjects out of books as she had been made to do at the Hall, reading the Classics with Aunt Emily, struggling with endless Arithmetic, Algebra and Geometry problems with the retired Governess, and doing hours of homework which usually consisted of copying out passages from a book.

Everything she did in Paris, everything she saw, seemed to sparkle as if it had a life of its own, and she knew that not only would she learn at break-neck speed, but also that every day new horizons were opening up before her eyes.

Then, just when she felt she was proficient in French, her father became enamoured of a very beautiful Italian *Contessa* and almost before Roberta realised what was happening they had moved to Italy.

First they stayed for several months in Venice, then in Rome, and lastly moved South to Naples.

It was here that the Earl's affection for the *Contessa* faded, and somebody new and very unusual attracted his attention instead.

Her name was Francine, and she was half-French, half-Arab.

She was to Roberta undoubtedly the most alluring and exotic woman she could ever have imagined, let alone met.

Francine had the sinuousness of a snake, and her large, almost black eyes seemed to hold all the allure and mystery of Africa.

The Earl was entranced by her and readily agreed that she should show him what she thought of as her own country.

Francine's mother had been an Algerian Princess, her father a French Diplomat stationed in Africa, who when his term of service was up had returned to his own country and to his wife who was waiting for him there.

Francine had been extremely well-educated and had been brought up as a Frenchwoman and not as an Arab as one might have expected.

She had married, which gave her freedom to escape from the confinements which her family placed upon her.

But whether she had left her husband, or he her, Roberta never knew.

She was now free, rich, and looking for excitement and adventure in the same way that the Earl was.

They certainly found it together, and as they accepted that Roberta should go with them, she found everything they did entrancing and far more informative than any lesson could possibly be.

Just as she had learnt French in France and Italian in Italy, now Roberta began to learn Arabic.

It was Francine who was able to teach her the different

dialects of the tribes, just as she could explain the history, the beliefs, and behaviour of the Arabs they met as they travelled through Algeria, Morocco, and down into Senegal.

To Roberta everything was fascinating, even the heat, the bad-tempered camels, the difficulties which frequently confronted them, and just as her father laughed at anything that occurred and thought it was a huge joke, so did she.

While Francine would throw up her hands, expostulate and rage at those who caused a disturbance, she too would laugh, even at the most uncomfortable disaster which befell them.

Then she would pull the Earl's head down to hers and kiss him so that they forgot everything but themselves.

It was a strange existence for a young girl, for they would go for weeks without seeing anybody but natives, and as Francine and her father had so much to say to each other they often forgot to address one word to her.

Roberta did not mind: She was so happy to be with him, and just as she was not jealous of Francine, it was a relief to know that she was not jealous of her.

Because Francine was used to a French household where everybody was accommodated from the youngest grandchild to the oldest grandparent, they all lived together, and she accepted Roberta in a way that none of her father's other mistresses had done.

She did not resent her, she did not worry about her, and it was doubtful if she even thought about her.

Roberta was just part and parcel of the happiness she was finding with the Earl, and he with her.

They journeyed over the mountains, they were guests of Arab Chieftains, or they camped at an oasis beside a well, slept through the hottest hours of the day, then moved on when it was cool.

It was all so fascinating, a story unfolding in front of Roberta's eyes, and there was always something new and exciting to be discovered.

Now suddenly Roberta knew that with her father's death it had come to an end.

chapter two

HAVING cried herself to sleep every night, by the time Roberta reached Marseilles she was very tired.

Then she told herself she should be ashamed to be her father's daughter if she could not do as he had suggested and make her journey to America an adventure.

He had been unconscious until the last moment before he died, when he had opened his eyes and looked at her as if, she thought, she was surrounded by a dazzling light.

Then he said very quietly:

"I love you—my darling!"

A moment later he stopped breathing.

She was not certain afterwards whether he was speaking to her or whether he thought she was her mother, but his words were a comfort and she had the feeling that his spirit would be with her wherever she went.

When Hassam and the camel-boys put him into his grave which they had dug just outside the oasis in the sand, she made no attempt to read the prayers of the Burial Service over him.

She only prayed in her heart that he would be happy wherever he was and he would still look after her.

The Arabs stood around and she felt there was sorrow in their dark eyes and that in their own way they had been very fond of her father.

Certainly they had all been with him ever since they had first come to Africa, and had been prepared to go wherever he wished to travel.

There was, as her father had anticipated, no difficulty in their taking her and the camels back to Algiers.

Hassam told them they would be paid when they got there, and when they reached the busy harbour town Hassam obtained what Roberta knew was a good price for the sale of the camels.

He, of course, took a percentage for himself, but that was the way in Arab countries, and she knew that he would not cheat her.

She was generous with the payments she made to all the men and especially to Hassam.

She could afford to because she found that her father had deposited a considerable sum of money in the Bank in Algiers as well as the papers he had spoken to her about.

Among them she found a copy of his Will in which he had left her everything he possessed.

This was of course, only his own private money, because the bulk of the fortune that went with the title, like the house and the estates, now belonged to the new Earl of Wentworth.

This was the Earl's nephew, the son of his younger brother with whom he had never been very friendly when he was alive, and the new Earl was one of the relatives who had disapproved very volubly of his raffish behaviour.

To know that he was now living in what had always been

her home made Roberta more determined than ever that she would not return to England and her grandmother but would do as her father suggested and find her Aunt Margaret.

It was however difficult to realise that she had only herself to rely upon, and after what had been nearly three years with her father, she found it hard to make her own decisions.

Yet just as she had reasoned out to herself that Gracie must go with her to Paris, so she knew now it would be a mistake to cross the Atlantic without a chaperon.

Her father had sent Gracie back from Paris with a sum of money that made her old eyes shine and, what was more important, a letter to his Solicitors to say she was to be given one of the cottages in the village where she had been born.

It was difficult for Gracie to express the happiness this gave her.

"There's no one in the whole world like His Lordship!" she said to Roberta. "Whatever they says about him, I know, and you mark my words, he'll get his reward in Heaven!"

"I hope so," Roberta replied finding it hard not to laugh.

"You look after him, M'Lady," Gracie went on almost fiercely. "He needs someone now your poor mother's dead, God rest her soul, and them other women as runs after him and flatters him, they've only got their eyes on his pockets, you can be sure of that!"

When Gracie had gone Roberta told her father what she had said and they laughed over it together.

At the same time, strange though it might seem, Roberta knew that the women who loved her father were not particularly avaricious where money was concerned.

They loved him as a man and were frantically jealous even of his daughter if she took up too much of his attention. But they were not the traditionally greedy courtesans who had caused such a sensation during the Second Empire.

In fact, when Roberta thought of it, she realised that the women her father loved were always in their way Ladies, and some sort of substitute for the loss of her mother.

Francine was different.

At the same time she was very proud of her Royal blood, and although her behaviour and tempermental storms would have undoubtedly shocked the Countess, she was always very conscious of her consequence.

She was also fastidious enough to do nothing in any way, to offend what the Earl considered good taste in a woman.

In fact, Roberta grew very fond of Francine and cried bitterly when she died.

It seemed impossible that anybody so vivacious, so filled with what the French call *'joie de vivre,'* should have gone and left nothing behind but the memory of her laughter.

'Papa would have felt very lonely without her if he had not become ill himself,' Roberta thought.

It was no consolation however to know that he had gone too and she was alone.

She booked a passage on a French ship to cross to Europe which was not very comfortable or clean but she had spent most of the journey in her cabin.

When she arrived at Marseilles, she asked to be taken to the best hotel.

She was well aware she might have had difficulty as a single woman in booking a room if they had not been impressed by her title.

When she had deposited her trunk, which had been left for safety at the Bank in Algiers, she had asked for a carriage to take her to the Shipping Office.

On the way she thought over her situation very carefully and remembered that once Francine had said:

"The French are snobs. Whenever I am in France I never forget to use the name I am entitled to use as my mother's daughter, whatever my father's shortcomings."

Accordingly, having asked to see the Manager of the Shipping Office, Roberta enquired in her excellent Parisian French about ships sailing for America.

"I am Lady Roberta Worth," she said, "and am unfortunately travelling alone as my father the Earl of Wentworth has just died in Africa. I should be grateful if you could inform me if there is a respectable couple taking the same journey who would be kind enough to chaperon me during the voyage. I should of course, be willing to pay for their services in protecting me."

The Manager of the Office, who had been, she thought, slightly off-hand when she first appeared, immediately became far more respectful.

He discovered that an English Clergyman, the Reverend Canon Bridges, and his wife would be aboard, and he was confident that if he spoke to them, they would be pleased to look after her.

Roberta left him to make the arrangements, and having learned that the ship, which was one of the largest of the French Liners on the Atlantic route, would be leaving in two days' time, went back to the Hotel to prepare herself for the voyage.

She had drawn a considerable sum of money from the Bank in Algiers, and she had learned from Francine how important it was when they were travelling to keep any money they possessed in a safe place.

It was Francine who had taught her how to sew some notes of large denominations into the hem of her skirt and to make herself a light lawn waist-band that could be worn next to her skin in which other money could be kept safely.

"It may seem strange," she had said. "At the same time, in Africa, anything lying about disappears mysteriously, and once it has gone there is no chance of ever seeing it again."

Roberta had listened, even though the necessity for concealing money did not concern her when her father paid for everything.

Now she was on her own, she knew she would be very stupid if she did not heed Francine's advice.

She therefore carried her money when she was crossing the Mediterranean round her waist, and as it was somewhat bulky she transferred the larger notes into the hem of the skirts which she was most likely to wear when she was at sea, and also when she reached America.

When she joined the ship early in the morning she was reassured to learn that Canon and Mrs. Bridges would be only too delighted to look after 'Lady Roberta Worth.'

The Canon was an elderly, genial, if rather pompous man who had been making a tour of the Protestant Churches in France on behalf of the Archbishop of Canterbury.

He and his wife were now going on to America where they were to meet the leaders of the Episcopal Church and they were both looking forward to the experience.

"I never thought we would go anywhere further from our house in Canterbury, than the English seaside," Mrs. Bridges told Roberta, "but it is God's will that we should travel, and it has been something I shall always remember."

She was a kindly woman who thought the sun rose and set on her husband's wishes, and was so narrow in her outlook that she eyed everything French with suspicion, including the food.

Roberta, who had grown used to the best French cooking with her father, found the food on board imaginative and at the beginning of the voyage, excellent.

The last days before they reached New Orleans the menu became somewhat monotonous, but still was served with a flair which only a French Chef could achieve.

The sea was very rough through the Bay of Biscay before they reached Cherbourg, where they called before setting off across the Atlantic.

Then they moved into smoother waters and Roberta was aware that had she not been safely under the wing of the Canon and his wife, she might have had trouble with some of the Frenchmen aboard, most of whom were going to America for commerical reasons.

She knew from the look in their eyes that they found her attractive, but she was wise enough not to wander about the deck alone, and to say that she could not dance in the evenings owing to the fact that she was in mourning.

She knew Mrs. Bridges approved of her behaviour, although she obviously thought it strange that Roberta should be travelling so far on her own.

"I hope somebody will be meeting you, Lady Roberta, when we dock at New Orleans," she said.

Because Roberta thought it was a mistake to say that nobody had any idea that she was coming, she only smiled and replied evasively:

"I hope so, but my aunt lives in California, which is a long way from the Mississippi."

"Of course, I know very little about America," Mrs. Bridges said, "and the Canon and I are rather nervous of what we shall find there, especially in places where there might be hostile Indians."

"I am sure it is safe, and your people will look after you," Roberta said consolingly.

She wished she could say the same to herself.

She had, in fact, written to her aunt and posted the letter from Marseilles, telling her that her father was dead and that she was coming out to visit her.

She had the feeling that the letter might arrive after she

did, or even by a strange coincidence might be travelling with the mail on the very ship in which she was now at sea.

"If Aunt Margaret will not help me," she told herself, "then I shall just have to go home again."

At the same time, the idea of facing the anger of her grandmother at her running away and hearing the same old denunciation of her father repeated and repeated, made her feel that any other existence would be preferable, however strange it might be.

As she did not know very much about America, nor had she been, as it happened in the past, particularly interested in it, New Orleans was a revelation.

She had not known what to expect but certainly not to find that it was, to all intents and purposes, another Paris on the other side of the world.

It was very hot for April, but after the winds and cold nights on the Atlantic Roberta felt as if the sunshine and the redolence of the City warmed her heart.

The first thing she noticed was the scent of coffee which pervaded the heavy air and was wafted from the great wharves and roasting ovens.

This seemed a part of Paris, like the houses themselves with their shutters and their balconies.

Then there were the strange smells from the Mississippi of river-ships and crayfish, of sugar, spices, bananas, rum and sawdust.

It seemed the right background for the flower-filled gardens, of black men sweating on the levees, for rich food swimming in butter, cream and wine, and the music of surging voices, soft, deep and resonant which were to be heard from dawn until dusk.

To Roberta it was all an enchantment after the barren desert, and so colourful that she felt she could never stop looking around her, finding everywhere scenes that any artist would be thrilled to paint.

"What a pity that Aunt Margaret does not live in New Orleans," she told herself.

She knew she had fallen in love with what seemed to her to be an enchanted City.

The food in the Hotel was delicious, but she longed to eat at one of the restaurants in the old town which the waiters told her provided as good, if not better, dishes than anything to be found in Paris.

When she went to the fish market she could quite believe it.

There she saw soft-shell crabs, crayfish, delicate little shrimps like tiny pink petals, trout, lobsters and oysters fresh from the sea.

'If only Papa were here! How much he would enjoy it!' Roberta thought.

She knew however it was wrong to linger and she must go on with her journey.

The letter from her aunt which she had found in Algiers had been written from Blue River, which she found, when she pored over a map aboard the French Liner, was a village some thirty or forty miles south of San Francisco.

The distance between New Orleans and California had in fact, frightened her, but she had learned that there were railways now all over America.

The Purser, who was very anxious to be friendly, told her that the Union-Pacific Railway would carry her from where they docked across Louisiana, Texas, New Mexico, Arizona and into California.

"You will be comfortable, Lady Roberta," he said "and quite safe."

"Do you mean from Indians?" Roberta asked, feeling

there might be a tremor in her voice such as there had been in Mrs. Bridge's.

"From Indians, and also from rival train-gangs who used to fight with each other ferociously."

"It must have been very frightening for the passengers!"

"It was," the Purser agreed, "but now all that is over, and I assure you that everybody keeps in their proper place, and you can sleep without hearing a pistol shot."

He laughed as if it was a joke, and offered to lend Roberta some books.

She read of how the rivalry between the great Railway owners like Commodore Vanderbilt, David Drew and George Low had often involved fierce battles in which a number of men had been wounded and even killed.

After she had lingered for a while in New Orleans she was well aware that as an unmarried woman some people eyed her with suspicion, and she knew that her father and certainly her mother would have said she was too young and too pretty to be on her own.

She therefore set off on what she knew would be a very long and tiring journey to find her aunt.

"One day I will come back," she promised as she had her last glimpse of New Orleans and said goodbye to the Mississippi River.

It seemed to her to have a romance all of its own.

Then as she consulted her map she found she was in the State of Louisiana and after that Texas.

After two or three days of watching the country out of the window and feeling the continuous vibration and noise of the wheels, Roberta began to feel that she was moving in a 'No-Man's-Land' between two points on the map and in consequence had lost her own identity.

She ate, she slept, she was looked after by a black attendant who treated her as if she was a small child who should be travelling with a Nanny.

She occasionally talked to the other travellers, who were mostly elderly, and she was thankful to say not particularly interested in her as a young woman.

As a safeguard she travelled First Class and she had an idea that things were very different in other parts of the train.

She noticed when they stopped at the stations that many of the passengers were tall and handsome with great white *sombreros* on their heads, and pistols on their hips hanging from belts heavy with silver nail heads which proclaimed they came from Texas.

They were certainly very impressive, but she had the feeling when she climbed back into her First Class Compartment further down the train that it was a good thing she was inaccessible.

There was one man she noticed in particular at every stop. She was not certain if he was a Texan, but he was as tall as they were and just as well proportioned.

He was extremely good looking which in him seemed fundamental rather than superficial, and in some subtle way he was different from the others.

His face was bronzed from the sun, his clothes were casual, and there was something which made her feel conscious of him even at a distance.

At every station he walked up and down alone and appeared to be deep in thought, but his body was lissom and attractive and he stood out on the platform filled with men.

She wondered if he would be surprised if she spoke to him, and then was shocked that she should even have thoughts of doing anything so unconventional and so imprudent.

Then at last, when Roberta felt as if she had been travelling for at least a year, they reached California.

Her book on the building of the Railways had told her that the great State was 770 miles long and about 250 miles wide, and was the world's greatest vineyard, orchard, and granary.

She had also read of the 'Gold Rush' which had taken place in 1849 and the mineral wealth of silver, platinum and plutonium which could be found in this wonderful land where everything 'turned to gold.'

'How wise Aunt Margaret was to come here,' she thought.

Because she had been so busy travelling Roberta had given very little time to concentrating on her aunt, and what she remembered of her.

All she could recall was hearing her talked about rather derisively.

Contrary to the family's expectations Lady Margaret had refused to accept any of the eligible young Englishmen who had proposed to her when she had made her début.

Riding and country pursuits had filled her life completely.

As her father the Earl was easy-going and had no wish to force his daughter to take a husband until she wished to do so, he had ignored his wife's constant cry that Margaret had to get married.

He let her enjoy herself at home, finding her company in the Hunting-field very much to his liking.

The Countess with her other children growing up and getting married was beginning to believe that Margaret was born to become an 'old maid,' when unexpectedly she fell in love.

Once a year her father and mother entertained the Vicars and Rectors of the Churches to which the Earl as Patron of the living, appointed the incumbent.

It was an event that nobody looked forward to, least of all the guests.

The Countess complained that their out-of-date evening clothes smelt of moth-balls, and the Earl said their wives were so shy and awkward it was impossible to get one word out of them.

One year the Vicar of their own village asked if he might bring with him an American Preacher who was staying with him as his guest.

The Countess somewhat reluctantly acquiesced and Clint Dulaine had come to dinner.

He was seated next to Lady Margaret, and afterwards looking back, her father and mother and those of her brothers and sisters who happened to be present, remembered how she had suddenly appeared to have a beauty they had never before noticed and to be more vivacious than anybody had ever known her to be.

Clint Dulaine had arranged to stay with the Vicar for two days. He remained for two weeks, and when he left Margaret went with him.

He declared himself with an American impetuosity for days after they had met.

When Margaret told her father she wished to marry an American Preacher he had not only been appalled by the idea but had forbidden her categorically ever to see the man again.

"I am not having any Bible thumpers in my family and least of all an American one!" he had declared. "You quite understand you are not to speak to this man or see him! If he tries to come into the house I shall order the servants to throw him out!"

Margaret appeared to listen to what her father had said, but she secretly met Clint in the woods and just as years

35

later her brother was to run away leaving a brief note behind him, she did the same.

One evening she said good-night to her parents in the same dutiful manner she had always done.

If they had been a little more observant they would have seen by the brightness of her eyes and the new beauty of her face that she was pulsating with excitement and joy.

Only when she had gone and they had no idea where, did they remember that she had seemed 'different.'

Margaret and Clint were married unconventionally at a Registry Office, and not until she was on her way to America did she write to her father and tell him that she was blissfully happy and looking forward to a new life in another part of the world.

The Earl with a shrug of his shoulders realised there was nothing he could do about it, but knew that he would miss Margaret when he was hunting, and the horses would miss her too.

Thinking back into her childhood Roberta could remember her Grandmother speaking in the same contemptuous tone about her daughter as she was later to speak about her son.

"It was very brave of Aunt Margaret," Roberta told herself, "and she will understand why I cannot go back to live with Grandmama and hear her saying such unkind things about Papa."

They reached a station, which she had been told was the nearest to Blue River Village, late in the afternoon.

It was a small station, and as she stepped out of the train Roberta could see at a glance there was nobody to meet her and knew as she might have expected, that her letter would not have arrived.

She might have sent her aunt a cable but she thought it would be difficult to explain her father's death in a few words, and the purpose of her journey.

A carrier was found to take her and her trunk into the village.

She gathered her appearance caused quite a commotion as they were obviously not used, in Blue River, to having anybody so smartly dressed or for that matter so young and pretty arriving unannounced.

The Carrier who called at the station to fetch the mail and a number of odd-looking parcels was fortunately unable to have her sitting beside him.

Had she done so, Roberta was quite certain he would have plied her with questions.

Instead there was a large, very fat, elderly woman who occupied the front of the cart as if by right, and who was so tired after her journey that she had no wish to talk.

The cart at the back had seats facing inwards and besides Roberta and her two trunks there were parcels and the sacks of mail.

There was also a hen-coop containing a cockerel and two hens which expressed their indignation and their dislike of travel the whole way from the station to the village.

The countryside however was lovely and it seemed to Roberta there was colour everywhere.

The shrubs were in bloom, the trees, many of which she did not recognise, were vivid with flowers, and as the land on either side of the road was cultivated the first green sprouts of Spring made it very picturesque.

"I am sure this is a happy land," she said to herself.

The words thrust away the apprehension she was feeling now that the journey had ended and she had to confront a relative with her presence without being sure whether or not she would be welcome.

If her aunt did not like her she would have to go home, as she had told herself not once but a dozen times during the sea voyage and on the train, until even thought seemed lost in the rumble of the wheels.

Because she was frightened she prayed:

"Please, Papa, wherever you are, make Aunt Margaret want me! I could not bear to go back after having come all this long way!"

She was still praying as the roofs of the village came in sight and she saw in the middle of them the spire of a rather ugly, newly built Church.

Some of the houses looked quite prosperous but there were others that were little more than shacks built in a haphazard manner on a flat piece of ground.

Beyond them was the river from which the village had taken its name.

She had told the Carrier, when he had agreed to take her to the village, where she wished to go, which was to The Haven, the address which had been written at the top of her Aunt's letter.

Now she had seen the Church she was sure that Mr. Dulaine, who had always been referred to disparagingly as an 'American Preacher,' was in fact a minister of the Episcopal Church.

Because of the way in which her relatives always spoke of him she had thought of him as one of the fanatics who she knew roamed the countryside, preaching to whoever would hear them, but having no authority apart from a burning faith to turn those who listened to them from sin to righteousness.

'At least Aunt Margaret is respectable,' Roberta thought.

She wondered why the Countess was not in this case, willing to forgive her daughter for running away and to accept her back into the bosom of the family.

It seemed strange that all the time she had been living

with her grandmother she had never once heard her mention her eldest daughter.

But it was part and parcel of the general attitude that anyone who defied the family could no longer be considered part of it.

"I suppose I am in the same position now," Roberta told herself ruefully.

The Carrier's horse came to a standstill and she saw in front of them a small grey house which was apparently built of wooden slats with a slate roof.

It had a porch which she knew was characteristic of American houses.

She climbed down from the cart and the Carrier, after handing the reins to the fat woman to hold, lifted her trunks down and followed her up a short path which led to the porch.

There were two steps up onto it, and he dumped down her trunk, accepted half-a-dollar without comment, and walked away without replying to her thanks.

It seemed slightly churlish, but Roberta had no time to think of him but only of what lay ahead.

The door in front of her had two glass panes in it, which it was impossible to see through.

There was no knocker, and although she looked for a bell she could not see one.

Then as she raised her hand to knock on the glass she heard a child screaming at the back of the house.

First it was one scream, then it was followed by a succession of them, each one louder than the last.

It was obvious that nobody could hear her knock above such a noise, and it also struck Roberta that perhaps the child had had an accident and was badly hurt.

Without really considering whether it was the right thing

to do or not, she pushed the door and found it was ajar.

Now as it opened the screams were absolutely deafening and she walked into a narrow hall with a steep staircase coming down on one side of it.

It was then she was aware that the screams came from the room directly in front of her, which she thought in most houses of this size would be the kitchen.

Having gone so far there was no turning back.

She walked on, opened the closed door, and found herself as she had expected, in what was obviously quite a large kitchen with two windows letting in the sunlight.

In the centre of it seated on a chair was a man with a beard beating a small boy with a cane.

He was bringing it down as hard as he could on the child's behind, and making him scream louder and louder at every stroke.

The child was small and the man seemed very big and menacing, and as Roberta saw the boy's face wet with tears, his mouth opening in anguish at what he was suffering, she walked forward to say sharply in a voice that was loud enough to be heard above the din:

"Stop that! Stop it at once!"

For a moment there was silence as if the noise had been turned off by a tap.

The man's arm was arrested in mid-air, and the child stared at her as if he could not believe what he saw.

In a voice that was quieter, but still positive, Roberta said:

"Excuse me, but I do not think any child should be submitted to such severe punishment!"

"Who are you and what do you want?" the man asked.

She realised as he spoke that he was educated, but as he was dressed only in his shirt-sleeves she had thought he was a servant.

As if he was suddenly aware that he had been reprieved, the small boy scrambled off the large man's knees, and rubbing his behind with his hands moved away until he was standing against the wall of the room and staring at Roberta, the tears still running down his cheeks.

He was a small, attractive-looking little boy, his head covered in golden curls, his eyes very blue in a thin, pale face.

The man still sat on the wooden chair and now he put his hands on his knees, one of them still holding the cane as he said:

"I asked you who you were and what you are doing here!"

"I am looking for my Aunt, Lady Margaret Dulaine."

"You'll not find her here," the man replied surlily.

"Why not?"

"Because she is in the Churchyard!"

Roberta stared, not understanding.

Then in a voice that trembled she asked:

"Are . . . are you saying that . . . Lady Margaret is . . . d–dead?"

The man still in the hard voice in which he had addressed her before said:

"Yes, dead, about six months ago."

"And her husband? Mr. Dulaine?"

"He went off. I've taken his place."

The man rose as he spoke.

"I cannot believe it!"

The words were spoken almost in a whisper, and because Roberta felt suddenly as if her legs would no longer carry her she sat down on the nearest chair.

She had never for a moment imagined that Aunt Margaret might possibly have left the village from where she had written two years earlier, let alone that she might have died.

"Who are you?"

The question was abrupt.

"I am Lady Margaret's niece. My name is Lady Roberta Worth."

"We've no use for titles in this country."

It was a blunt statement and Roberta did not answer.

Yet as if in spite of himself she commanded his respect, the man with the beard put on a black clerical coat that was lying over a chair.

When he had shrugged himself into it he looked across the room at the small boy who was still staring at Roberta and rubbing his behind and said:

"Get out, you little varmint! And if I find you stealing the food again I'll give you the rest of the beating you've escaped now!"

The small boy gave a gasp and rushed out through the door at the back of the room which he slammed noisily behind him.

The man frowned, but he did not say anything.

Looking at Roberta who seemed almost to have collapsed in the chair in which she was sitting, he poured her out a glass of water from a jug standing on the sink and handed it to her.

She took it from him saying:

"Thank . . . you."

She realised as she spoke that her voice seemed to come from very far away.

She drank the water and the coolness of it seemed to take away the feeling that she was beginning to float on the air and there was a darkness coming up from the floor.

The man stood watching her until as he was satisfied that she had revived a little, he asked:

"Where have you come from?"

"From Algiers. My father, the Earl of Wentworth, died

there, and he suggested I should come and stay with my aunt. He had, of course, no idea she had died."

"From Algiers!"

It was obvious that the length of her journey impressed him.

"Are you the Vicar of this Parish?"

"I'm the Minister."

"Yes, of course, I had forgotten that is what you would be called in America."

"What are you going to do with yourself?"

The Minister had a hard voice with no kindness or compassion in it.

"I suppose the first thing I must do is find somewhere where I can stay the night," Roberta replied.

There was silence. Then after a moment the Minister said reluctantly:

"I suppose you could stay here."

"Thank you, that is a very kind offer."

"Then what do you intend to do?"

"I . . . I have not had time to think about it . . . but if Aunt Margaret is dead, and you have no idea where I can find Mr. Dulaine . . . then I suppose I must go home to England."

Again there was silence. Then after a minute the Minister said:

"Can you work?"

"Work?" Roberta repeated.

"Cook, clean, look after a house?"

The words came out abruptly.

Roberta was just about to retort that as she had money there was no necessity for her to perform such menial tasks.

Then just as she was about to open her lips she saw the small boy peering through the window of the back door.

His face was still streaked with tears, the sun was shining

on his fair curls, and he looked, she thought, almost like a small, unhappy angel peeping down on her from the clouds of Heaven.

As she looked at him she remembered he had been beaten because he had stolen food.

She was quite certain from the hollowness of his cheeks and the thinness of his neck that he was far from being well-fed.

Impulsively she asked the question which came to her lips.

"Who is the small boy you were chastising when I arrived?"

She had the feeling after she had spoken that the Minister wanted to tell her to mind her own business.

Instead he said gruffly:

"There was an accident on the railroad near Blue River. His parents were both killed and your aunt adopted him."

"Adopted him!" Roberta exclaimed. "Then why did Mr. Dulaine not take him with him?"

"He left me a message to say he would come for him when he had a home."

As if the Minister was aware that Roberta was waiting to hear more, he said, almost as if the words were dragged from him:

"He has gone back to preaching, moving from place to place. I think he's a fool, but it is his way of trying to forget."

"You mean he wanted to forget my aunt because he was upset when she died."

"They had been together for a long time, but sensible men do not give up on their jobs and wander around aimlessly."

"And you said you would look after the boy?"

"If I had any sense," the Minister replied, "I would put him in an Orphanage where he belongs. He's always stealing and lying, and I'll beat the Devil out of him, if it's the last thing I do!"

Roberta's lips tightened.

Then she forced herself not to utter the words that were in her mind. Instead she said quietly:

"You asked me if I could work. I am considered a good cook."

As she spoke she thought of the times she had cooked for her father these last two years when they were on their travels.

Francine, like most French women, was a natural cook but she disliked doing it, so she taught Roberta how to cook many of the dishes which she and her father had found most delicious when they were living in Paris.

Because Roberta liked cooking, nine times out of ten she managed alone, and she grew extremely proficient at making delicious meals out of anything they carried with them and they could find where they camped.

"Yes, I can cook," she repeated aloud.

"Very well," the Minister said, "I will engage you as Housekeeper. You'll find it cheaper than paying for a roof over your head, and we'll talk about what I will pay you for your services later when I see what they are worth."

The way he spoke made Roberta know perceptively that, if he could get away with it, he would pay her nothing.

Now she was beginning to understand why the small boy looked half-starved and why he stole.

Resolutely she rose from the chair in which she had been sitting.

"If you will show me where I can sleep," she said, "and help me in with my trunks which are on the verandah, I will try to prepare you something for supper."

She knew by the expression on the Minister's face that he was pleased at her acquiescence.

She was in fact, certain he was gloating to himself over his cleverness in acquiring a maid-servant on the cheap.

chapter three

"I WILL not be back for luncheon."

Without any more formal polite goodbye, the Minister stomped out of the house, down the steps of the verandah and started to walk away towards the Church.

Roberta gave a sigh of relief.

She found that every moment she was with him she disliked him more, and it was with the greatest difficulty that she prevented herself from contradicting the statements he made which were opposed to everything in which she believed.

She had realised at supper last night how mean he was to the small boy whose name, she had discovered, was Daniel.

"Mama called me Danny," he told Roberta when he came into the kitchen before supper.

"Then that is what I will call you," she said, "and you shall call me Aunt Roberta."

He smiled at her and said:

"That's a nice name."

"I am glad you like it."

Roberta realised however that he was looking longingly at what she was cooking, and she took a hot scone, which the Americans called a biscuit, from the oven and gave it to him.

He looked at it incredulously before he asked:

"Is this for me?"

"Yes," she said, "you can eat it as it is, or you can put some butter or jam on it."

He made a sound of excitement which she thought was very pathetic. Then without waiting for butter or jam he began to gobble the scone, which made her realise how hungry he was.

Without deliberately watching him she noticed that when he had eaten three-quarters of it, he slipped the rest into the pocket of his trousers.

She did not say anything but went on cooking, feeling there was little enough in the larder for two people, let alone three.

She however made an appetising dish of some pieces of meat and garnished it with potatoes.

She knew that would not be enough but managed with a great deal of ingenuity to make a vegetable soup to start the meal.

When she set it before the Minister he asked:

"Is this all we are having for supper?"

"No, of course not," Roberta replied. "There is a meat dish to follow the soup."

"Two dishes!" he said critically. "I hope you are not being extravagant!"

"There was very little in the larder," Roberta replied, "and I am sure, Minister, a big man like you needs proper feeding."

She thought her flattery made the Minister preen himself before he said:

"I certainly need feeding with the right food, but I have to be careful. I have trouble with my heart."

By the end of supper she was quite certain that if he had a heart there was no compassion in it for anybody except himself.

She was appalled at how little of the main dish he gave to Danny. In fact, it was little more than a spoonful of the meat and two spoonfuls of potatoes.

She received the same, and he ate everything that was left.

Because she felt it was very scanty fare and Danny was hungry, she had contrived with a great deal of ingenuity to prepare some toasted cheese to finish the supper.

Again the Minister seemed surprised but he ate it up, and she thought he looked scornful because she had given Danny the same amount as she gave him.

He did not say anything until the meal was over. Then after an elaborate Grace he said in a menacing voice:

"Now remember, Daniel, if I find you stealing or lying again, I'll not only beat you, but I'll take steps to send you to the Orphanage where you'll be forced to behave yourself!"

Roberta saw Danny shiver as the Minister spoke and knew that the threat of the Orphanage was a Bogey-man which was held over his head continually. In fact, she noticed that he went paler than he was already whenever it was mentioned.

When the Minister left the kitchen for his Study she started to clear away the dishes.

She had made a small toasted cheese for herself but had eaten only half of it. This she threw into a bin by the sink.

She had turned her back to take the cloth from the table

when something made her look over her shoulder.

She saw Danny retrieve what she had left of the toasted cheese from the dustbin, and putting it into his pocket he ran from the kitchen out across the garden at the back of the house.

She had not had time to explore before supper, but now she saw there was a considerable area of garden behind the house and beyond was a clump of trees.

They looked very lovely against the evening sky which was full of colour.

On an impulse she left the dishes she was washing up and walked across the garden towards the trees where she knew Danny had gone, but when she reached them there was no sign of the small boy.

She stood listening.

Then she heard his voice, very low, talking to somebody.

Moving silently in the thin slippers she had worn for supper, Roberta moved in the direction of the sound and peeped through some bushes.

Danny was sitting on the ground and beside him was a large dog which he was feeding with the pieces of food he had saved from supper.

She did not speak or move, but the mere fact that she was there must somehow have attracted his attention.

He looked up, saw her and gave a little scream of terror.

"Hide, Columbus, hide!" he said frantically and the dog slipped away into the bushes so quickly that it was almost as if he had never been there.

Only as Danny stood staring at Roberta with frightened eyes and she saw he was trembling did she move through the bushes towards him.

"Is that your dog?" she asked as she reached him. "I love dogs, so do not send him away."

"You love . . . dogs?"

He repeated the words in a voice that trembled and she said:

"I used to have a dog of my own when I lived in the country in England, and I loved him very much."

There was silence. Then Danny said:

"If Mr. Minister sees Columbus he says he'll shoot him!"

Roberta sat down on the ground at Danny's side.

"I am sure he was only frightening you."

"He really will!" Danny declared. "That's why I have to hide Columbus here."

He looked at her in sudden terror as he asked:

"You will not tell... Mr. Minister?"

"No, of course I will not tell him," Roberta said. "It shall be our secret. Call your dog back, and let me meet him."

Danny hesitated a moment as if he feared she was tricking him. Then he gave a low whistle and Columbus came creeping out from beneath the bushes.

He had a spaniel's head but was obviously a mongrel. His coat was very long besides being ragged and untidy from the rough way in which he was living, and he also had a big curly tail.

He had the liquid, loving eyes of an English spaniel, and he nuzzled his nose against Danny in a way which told Roberta without words how much they meant to each other.

"This is Columbus," Danny said.

"Why do you call him that?"

"My Mama said Christopher Columbus discovered America, and Columbus discovered me!"

"Then I think that is a very good name you have given him."

"Mama let me keep him in the house and he used to sleep on my bed," Danny said, "but Mr. Minister hates dogs and told Columbus to go away and not come back."

51

Roberta pressed her lips together to stop herself from saying how cruel she thought that was.

Now as she looked at Columbus she could see the dog was very thin, and knew that just as Danny was suffering from what was almost starvation, Columbus was suffering in the same way.

"I tell you what we will do, Danny," she said, "I will make a proper meal for Columbus every day and you can bring it out here to him, but we will have to be careful that 'Mr. Minister,' as you call him, does not find out."

"If he does find out," Danny said, "he won't allow you to feed Columbus, and then he'll die."

Roberta realised this was a very real fear and she said:

"I am sure he does not mean to do anything so wrong, but your father will be coming back soon."

"He said he would come back," Danny said in a very small voice, "but perhaps he has walked for miles and miles and forgotten about me."

"I am sure he will not do that," Roberta said. "In the meantime, I will see that you have more food to eat and Columbus has a proper meal at least once a day."

She thought as she spoke she was quite certain if this was to happen she would have to pay for it, and she was glad to think she had plenty of money left even after her long journey.

What was more, once she was settled, she could write to her father's Bank in England and get them to send her more money in America.

But first she must be quite certain that she would still be there when the money arrived.

"If you come back to the house now," she said. "I will find something for Columbus to eat and tomorrow we will give him a big meal which he will really enjoy."

She knew as Danny put his arms around Columbus and hugged him how much this meant to him.

When she walked back hand-in-hand with the small boy she persuaded him to talk to her about her aunt whom he called his mother, and Clint Dulaine whom he called his father.

It was obvious he did not remember his real mother and father, and she did not like to ask too many questions about them.

After they had taken Columbus all the scraps there were in the kitchen, and there were pitifully few of them, Roberta sent Danny up to bed and took him a hot drink she had made from some chocolate she had bought at one of the stations where she had stopped during her train journey.

He drank every drop and when he had finished he said:

"Now the pain in my tummy's gone."

"Is that what you have been having every night?" Roberta asked.

"And in the day. It's a nasty pain."

"That is something we must stop you from having again," Roberta said.

She bent down to kiss him, and he put his arms around her neck.

He had grown sleepy, but he asked:

"Did Mama send you from God?"

"I think she must have done," Roberta replied, and she felt the tears prick her eyes.

She was to learn more about her aunt the next morning soon after the Minister had left.

Danny was waiting for her and she was just going to ask him where she could go to buy some food for luncheon, when without knocking a woman walked in through the back door.

She was a middle-aged woman, rather gaunt-looking, and Roberta realised she was staring at her in an extremely hostile manner.

The woman did not speak, but merely glanced around the kitchen, then stood with her hands on her hips, staring at her.

"Good morning!" Roberta said after a moment.

"It may be a good morning to you," the woman replied, "but I've just come to see who's done me out of me job!"

"Done you out of your job!" Roberta exclaimed.

"You know what I'm talking about!" the woman replied aggressively. "I've just met the Minister in the street and he tells me he's got a new Housekeeper and doesn't require my services any longer."

The woman spoke the last words in an affected tone as if she was copying the Minister's refined accent.

"I am sorry," Roberta said. "I had no idea anybody worked here."

"For three years," the woman said. "Three years and never missed a day, except to have my last child. Now in you've come, and out I go!"

"Perhaps you will tell me your name," Roberta said. "Mine is Roberta Worth, and Mrs. Dulaine was my aunt."

"So that's who you are! Everybody in the village was wondering who you might be when you got off the train," the woman said. "Well, all I can say is that Mrs. Dulaine would never have treated me in the way I've been treated now."

"I can quite believe that!" Roberta said. "And there is a great deal I want to hear about my aunt who I did not know had died before I arrived here. So, please, will you sit down and I think there is a little coffee left, but nothing else."

For the moment she thought the woman was going to refuse, then as if she was too curious to go away she pulled out a chair and sat down at the table.

Roberta fetched the coffee which was left over from breakfast and poured her out a cup, realising as she did so that there was none left for herself.

She looked at the empty coffee-pot a little ruefully and the woman said:

"He wouldn't have left that if he could have helped it. He's that mean!"

"Are you speaking about the Minister?"

"I am! And I'm not afraid to say so. Things was very different when your aunt was alive, I can tell you that."

"That is what I want to hear about," Roberta said, "but first will you tell me your name?"

"Mrs. Srubotski," the woman replied, "but most people can't pronounce it, so they calls me 'Mrs. Ski.'"

Roberta laughed.

"It is a rather difficult name."

"It's Polish," Mrs. Ski explained briefly. "My father and mother came here in the 'Gold Rush.' But I don't remember much about it."

"Tell me about my aunt," Roberta begged, feeling that if they once got onto the subject of the Gold Rush it would be impossible to get the information she really wanted.

Sipping the coffee as if she enjoyed it Mrs. Ski was very voluble about how everybody had loved Mr. and Mrs. Dulaine, and how finding there was no proper place of worship he had built the Church.

"It was just like her," Mrs. Ski went on, "to adopt young Daniel. Fifteen people were killed when the train came off the rails and his real father and mother were among them!"

"How old was he then?" Roberta asked.

"I thinks he was about two," Mrs. Ski replied.

"And how old is he now?"

"Seven. The Minister's got his Birth Certificate somewhere in his desk if you ask to see it."

They talked for some time about her aunt, then Roberta said:

"Mrs. Ski, I have an idea! I agreed to be Housekeeper here, not knowing the Minister had anybody else, because after I learnt that my aunt was dead I could not think quickly where I could go, or what I could do."

Mrs. Ski nodded as if she understood.

"What I am going to suggest," Roberta went on, "is that you will come and clean the house as you always have and I will pay you, but there is no need to let the Minister know about it."

Mrs. Ski stared at her in astonishment.

"You mean you can afford to do that?"

"I can afford it for the time being," Roberta replied, "and quite frankly, I would be very grateful for your help as I do not like housework, although I rather enjoy cooking."

"I don't mind cooking when there's something to cook!" Mrs. Ski said. "But that old meanie won't buy enough to keep a mouse alive!"

"Danny is definitely under-nourished," Roberta said and looked out through the kitchen door to where Danny was playing in the garden.

"That's true," Mrs. Ski replied. "He's real cruel to that boy! Always beating and a—cursing him, and telling him he'll send him to an Orphanage. It's not right, and if she knew about it, your aunt would turn in her grave!"

"I am sure she would," Roberta said quietly. "So I must stay here at any rate for a little while, for Danny's sake and . . ."

She almost added: ". . . and his dog," but thought perhaps it would be a mistake to say too much to Mrs. Ski in case she talked.

In a more practical tone she said:

56

"The first thing you must tell me is where I can buy some food and how much I may spend."

"If the Minister's paying, so little you could put it in your eye and not notice it," Mrs. Ski replied.

"As I do not know the shops or the way there," Roberta said, "I should be very grateful if you would buy what we need for today and later I will try to come to some agreement with the Minister."

Mrs. Ski looked doubtful, but Roberta had the idea that she was longing to be the first to tell them in the village that she was Mrs. Dulaine's niece.

Roberta wrote out a list of her requirements and when she added: 'Meat bones and any scraps which the Butcher will dispose of cheaply.' Mrs. Ski looked at her sharply and asked:

"You're not intending to feed that dog of young Daniel's?"

"You know about Columbus?"

"Of course I knows! But the Minister says he'll shoot him if he finds him in the house!"

"Surely he does not really intend to do anything so outrageous?"

"He will an' all!" Mrs. Ski replied. "He hates that boy and he loathes dogs!"

"Then we must certainly feed him without the Minister being aware of it," Roberta said resolutely.

She went to her bedroom and taking some money from where she had hidden it came back and gave it to Mrs. Ski.

"You're not spending all this at once?" Mrs. Ski asked.

"What I am going to suggest," Roberta said, "is that you buy enough for today, which is Saturday and tomorrow, as I presume on Sunday the shops will be closed. Then on Monday we can see how much is wanted for the rest of the week."

Mrs. Ski stared at her.

"You're trusting me to do that?"

Roberta smiled.

"But of course! You looked after my aunt, and I hope you will look after me too."

Mrs. Ski did not speak for a moment. Then she said:

"That man wouldn't trust me with a dime in case I took it off him!"

They both knew of whom she was speaking, and Roberta realised that the Minister had hurt the woman whom her aunt had trusted.

Impulsively she put her hand on Mrs. Ski's and said:

"We both have to think of what my aunt would have wanted. Because she loved Danny we have to make up for the love he has lost."

Mrs. Ski looked at her and Roberta thought there was a suspicion of tears in her eyes as she said:

"Your aunt was a Lady, and you're a Lady too!"

"Thank you."

As Roberta spoke she knew she had never received a more sincere compliment.

When Mrs. Ski had fetched the food and cleaned the house, Roberta knew she was worth every cent of the very small amount of money she asked for, for her services.

It was certainly a joy to be able to concentrate on the cooking and nothing else, and it gave her a feeling of pleasure she had not known since her father died when she saw Danny finish up a large plate of meat at luncheon.

She knew he was happy because before they ate she had prepared a huge meal for Columbus.

Danny had watched the dog eat at first ravenously as if he was afraid that the food would vanish before he could consume it, then more slowly until his bowl was empty.

Then he stood wagging his tail and licking Danny's hand

as if to express his gratitude, and Roberta knew that it would be impossible for her to leave them to their fate.

She therefore decided that until Clint Dulaine's return she would feel it her responsibility to take her aunt's place in Danny's life.

She soon learnt it was going to be very difficult, because as soon as the Minister returned the atmosphere in the house changed from one of happiness into one of fear.

Danny seemed to shrink into himself as the large man came up the steps onto the verandah, and Roberta thought the Minister seemed to be looking around as if to find something wrong which he could complain about.

Mrs. Ski had however left everything spotlessly clean and in its proper place.

Roberta knew as she stood cooking a delicious meal that the aroma of it was making the Minister sniff suspiciously as he entered the kitchen.

"What are you cooking?" he demanded. "If it is something expensive, I'll not pay for it!"

"The chicken was cheap today," Roberta replied, "and I think you will enjoy this one made with a sauce which I learnt in France."

She thought the Minister was going to say that that was the last thing he wanted to eat, but he was greedy and she knew by the expression on his face that what he could smell cooking was making him feel hungry.

As if he had to be unpleasant to somebody he looked at Danny and asked:

"Has that child behaved himself today? Has he been polite to you?"

"He has been very sweet and very helpful," Roberta said firmly. "He has washed his hands ready for supper, and so if you are going to do the same, you had better hurry or

59

the chicken will be over-cooked."

The Minister looked at her as if he could hardly believe what he was hearing.

Five minutes later they were all seated round the table.

Roberta however had learnt her lesson from the night before and this time she carved the chicken in the kitchen and gave half of it to the Minister before she divided what was left between Danny and herself.

He did not say anything, but she had the feeling that in the case of a joint of meat the Minister would insist on his right to do the carving.

But for the moment he was engaged in enjoying not only the chicken but the excellent salad that went with it, the potatoes she had fried until they were golden brown and the hot biscuits, light as thistledown.

They were not very different from the scones her father had enjoyed when she had the right ingredients to cook them, and as he had always said:

"No one, unless they have Scottish blood in their veins, can bake a really good scone."

The Minister paid her no compliments, but he ate everything that was put in front of him, including the light lemon souffle which followed with a chocolate sauce, and only when Danny had gone happily off to bed did he say to Roberta:

"Now, Miss Worth, we had better get down to 'brass tacks'. You're a good cook, I'm not denying that, but I am a poor man and I cannot afford fancy meals."

"But you enjoy them!"

"A Minister can only spend what he can afford."

"As I am a very good Housekeeper," Roberta said quietly, "let us wait until the end of the week. Then I will tell you what I have spent and if it is too much, then I must try to do better."

She knew as she spoke that the Minister was calculating that what he was saving, as he thought, on Mrs. Ski's services, he could spend on food.

At the same time, his meanness made him say:

"I'm not spending what I've not got, and it's a mistake for the boy to think he can eat like a horse when he is living on my charity."

"He is very small," Roberta said, "and I feel sure that Mr. Dulaine, when he returns, will recompense you for his keep."

"*If* he returns!" the Minister answered. "The last time I heard of him he was high up in the Rocky Mountains. If you ask me, the man's insane!"

Roberta was still for a moment. Then she asked:

"Are you saying you think he will not come back?"

"Why should he?" the Minister replied. "I've taken his place and he's not turning me out!"

There was no answer to this and Roberta suddenly felt as if she had been caught in a trap.

Then she told herself sensibly there was no point in coming to any quick decisions.

At the same time, she had no wish to spend the rest of her life, or many years of it, in Blue River.

She expected when she went to Church on Sunday that people would look at her with curiosity, but she was not prepared for the welcome she received from almost every woman in the congregation.

The Minister read the Service in what Roberta felt was a hard, unsympathetic voice, and when it came to the Sermon it was a tirade against sin, in which he described with what she thought with relish, the punishments sinners would receive after they were dead.

When the Service was over and Roberta started to walk down the aisle with Danny she was besieged by people wishing to shake her hand and to tell her how fond they had been of her aunt.

She was also asked a lot of questions as to why she had come such a long way to visit her relative, how long she intended to stay, and if it had been a great shock to realise that her aunt was dead.

As she left the Church and started to walk back to The Haven, she received dozens of invitations to ''drop in for a cup of coffee,' and what she knew would be a long interrogation about herself.

She had worn the plainest clothes she had with her, but as the gown and the short jacket that went over it had been bought in Paris she certainly looked very different from every other woman in Blue River.

Her bonnet too, although she had taken off the flowers and feathers which decorated it, had a Parisian *chic* which nothing could alter.

She could understand how in such a small place she would be a topic of conversation for a good deal more than the proverbial nine days.

Roberta thought that the Minister resented that his Parishioners had been interested in her, and therefore was more disagreeable than usual.

Once again he expressed the hope as their supper ended that she had not been extravagant and pointed out that it was the first time there had been cream on his table and as he was not a millionaire it had better be the last.

Because he was so surly and disagreeable Roberta knew that Danny was trembling and he had even made the food lose its taste.

"My mother always said, Minister," she remarked, "that if anyone was cross or unhappy at mealtimes they would suffer from indigestion. I am sure with your heart problem you ought to be very careful not to upset yourself, and try to forget all controversial subjects until you have finished eating."

The Minister looked at her in astonishment. Then he asked:

"Are you teaching me, young woman, how to behave?"

Roberta gave him a little smile.

"I was only thinking of what might happen in Blue River if they were left without a Minister."

She knew he wanted to forbid her to talk to him in such a manner but since the mere thought of his heart frightened him he put his hand on his chest.

He drank down a cup of coffee almost at a gulp as if to prevent himself from expressing the anger he was undoubtedly feeling.

When she went upstairs to say good-night to Danny he said:

"You are very brave, Aunt Roberta. You are not frightened of Mr. Minister like me and Columbus."

"There is no need to be frightened of him."

"But I *am* frightened!" Danny protested. "He beat me every day until you came, and I am still very, very frightened that he will find Columbus."

"I will protect you and Columbus," Roberta promised.

She spoke more prophetically than she knew.

It was the end of the week and while Danny was at School she had accepted the invitation of a woman who lived a few doors away who said she wanted to talk to her about her aunt.

She had been entertained with coffee in the garden, and her hostess had regaled her with a mass of anecdotes about her aunt and Clint Dulaine.

"They were a fine-looking couple together," she said, "and it was obvious how happy they were, even though your aunt was an Englishwoman."

Roberta laughed.

"Are not Englishwomen supposed to be happy?"

"Not living the sort of life Mrs. Dulaine endured when she first came to America!"

"Tell me about it," Roberta begged.

"Well, a Preacher is a Preacher," was the answer, "and while Clint preached and walked, and walked and preached, your aunt went with him and the people who met them said they were just like love-birds and as happy as the day was long."

"I like to hear that," Roberta smiled. "I often wondered if my aunt ever regretted having run away from her home, from everything that was conventional and of course, by those standards, very grand."

She then went on to describe what Worth Park was like, and how the life her aunt had lived there had been much the same as that which her father had found so boring.

"Now that Mrs. Dulaine is dead, will you be going back?" Roberta was asked.

It was a question she had asked herself almost every night this last week.

It was something she knew she ought to do, but it was difficult to know how she could take Danny with her, and if, even though he disliked him, the Minister would let him go.

It was a question she had been too nervous to broach so far, and walking back to The Haven she thought that when the moment was propitious she could perhaps find out if the Minister would really be pleased to be rid of Danny.

She walked up the steps of the verandah, then as if what had happened a week ago was repeating itself, she heard Danny screaming in terror.

She pushed upon the door and ran towards the kitchen.

As she went into it she saw Danny, not as she had expected being beaten, but was standing at the far end across the corner, his arms outstretched, screaming at the top of his voice.

"No! You shan't kill him—you shan't!"

Cowering behind him, trying to make himself as small a possible was Columbus, and standing in front of them with a shot-gun in his hand was the Minister.

His face was crimson with rage as he pointed the gun at Danny shouting at the top of his voice:

"Get out of my way! I told you if you brought that dog into the house I would shoot him, and that is what I intend to do!"

Roberta did not hesitate.

She rushed forward, throwing herself against the Minister, caught hold of the shot-gun with both hands, and turned it upwards.

"You will not shoot that dog!" she said. "I will not allow you to do so."

"How dare you interfere with me!" the Minister roared. "I will shoot the dog and the boy too, if you do not get out of my way!"

"You are mad!" Roberta retorted.

As she spoke with both hands on the gun she tried to drag it away from him.

He struggled with her and must have pulled the trigger as he did so, for there was a loud explosion.

The gun-shot hit the ceiling and the plaster fell down on Danny's head, which although it did not hurt him made him scream in terror.

Then, so suddenly that Roberta almost fell backwards, the Minister loosened his hold on the gun and put his hand up to his throat.

He gave a strange gurgle which was unlike any sound Roberta had ever heard before and collapsed onto the floor.

He was a big man and he fell slowly.

When finally his whole body was down he made that strange, horrifying sound again before there was complete silence.

Roberta stood looking at him, the gun in her hands, feeling that what had happened could not be true but just a figment of her imagination.

Then Danny crept to her side and looked up to ask:

"Have you—shot him?"

"No," Roberta replied. "I think he has had a . . . heart-attack."

Her voice sounded as if it came from a long distance away, then as the gun felt heavy she put it down on the kitchen table.

Slowly, because she was frightened, she knelt down beside the Minister and knew as she did so that he was dead.

She had seen too many people dying in Africa not to recognise the signs, and there was no need for her to feel his heart or his pulse to know that he had stopped breathing.

His condition which she had thought he had exaggerated had finally killed him.

She got to her feet and as she did so Danny flung his arms around her waist and hid his face in her skirt.

"It is . . . all right, darling," Roberta said unsteadily.

Danny only held her tighter and she realised he was crying.

"If he is—dead," he said, "they'll take me—away. Mr. Minister said if anything—happened to—him they would—take me to the—Orphanage."

As he spoke Roberta knew this was very likely true.

It flashed through her mind that as she was only just nineteen it was very unlikely the authorities would think her a suitable Guardian for Danny, even if she said she would take him to England with her.

It was then, almost as if her father was advising and directing her, that she knew that if she was to save Danny she would have to take him away at once, before anybody was aware of what had happened.

Afterwards she was quite certain that with his facility for organization it was her father who had helped her.

She picked up the gun, removed the empty cartridge case, and returned it to its place in the passage. She brushed up the pieces of plaster which had fallen from the ceiling, hoping nobody would look up and see the mark and suspect what had happened.

Then she told Danny to change into his best clothes and put his other things away for her to pack on the bed.

"Take Columbus up to your bedroom and stay there," she said, "until I come to fetch you."

He looked at her, the tears on his cheeks making him look very much the same as he had the first day she had seen him.

"You will not go—away without—me?" he asked.

"Of course not," she answered. "We are going to go away together, Danny, where nobody will find us, and no one will ask questions about how the Minister died."

"He was—going to—kill Columbus," Danny said, a tremble in his voice.

"I know," Roberta agreed, "but he cannot do that now, and you do not wish to stay here, now knowing where you should go or who you should be with."

As if he knew that was the most crucial question of all Danny said:

"I want to be—with you—Aunt Roberta."

"I have promised to look after you," Roberta replied, "but we have to be very clever and very quick, so do as I say and go to your room."

He did so and Roberta went to the Minister's Study.

She opened several drawers of the desk before she found what she was seeking which was Danny's Birth Certificate.

In the envelope with it was a wedding-ring which she guessed had belonged to his mother and had been taken from her finger before she was buried.

As she looked at it she had a sudden idea.

She slipped the ring onto the third finger of her left hand and found that although it was a little tight, it fitted her.

Then she opened Danny's Birth Certificate.

He had been born to a Mr. and Mrs. Boscombe in New Orleans on the 3rd September 1878, his name was Daniel, but there was no address.

Putting the Birth Certificate into her pocket she shut the drawer, then opened the others.

She found nothing there which concerned her aunt or her husband, so she shut them up again and went to her own room.

It was difficult to decide what she should take with her and what she should leave behind.

Finally she packed what the Americans called a 'grip' which was a very light case which could hold a number of her thinnest gowns and under-clothes without making it too heavy for her to carry.

It was sad to leave behind so many of the pretty things which her father had bought her in Paris.

But she had a feeling they were now not only too small, but also because they had been so long in Africa many of them were too young for her, especially in what she had decided should be her new role.

When she had packed and had put on the gown she considered most suitable for travelling, she went into Danny's bedroom.

He was sitting on his bed cuddling Columbus, and she realised from the way he looked at her that he was still shocked and also very frightened at what was happening.

She sat down beside him and patted Columbus before she said:

"Now, darling, I want you to listen to me very carefully. We are going away and I do not yet know exactly where we are going. But because I want to look after you, as I promised I would do, and Columbus, I am going to pretend that I am your mother, your real mother."

"My mother who was—killed in the—Railroad accident?" Danny asked.

"That is right," Roberta agreed. "I have your Birth Certificate which tells me how old you are, and because I am afraid people might try to take you away from me and say that because I am unmarried I am not a fit person to look after you, I want you to call me 'Mama,' and make everybody who meets us believe I am your real mother."

There was silence for a moment, then Danny smiled.

"I'd like you to be my Mama," he said. "I love you . . . Aunt Roberta!"

"And I love you, darling," Roberta said, "but unless we are not to get into a lot of trouble, we have to be very clever."

She thought Danny understood and added:

"This is an adventure, but a secret one. Do you understand?"

"I will say you are my Mama," Danny said, "and Columbus would say so too, if he could speak."

"Columbus understands all about how to keep secrets," Roberta said, "so you have to be clever, like him."

"Can we go now?" Danny asked.

"Not until later so that nobody will notice us," Roberta replied. "I am going downstairs now to get us something to eat, but you are to stay here until I call you."

She had no wish for him to see the Minister again, so

she collected some food from the kitchen, heated coffee for herself, and carried it all to the Study where she put it on a side-table.

Then having closed the kitchen door, she called Danny, and he and Columbus ate what she had prepared although Roberta felt herself unable to swallow a single mouthful.

They set off finally when the shadows were long and she knew that most people in the village would be sitting down to their evening meal.

It would have been very foolish to walk down the main street where they could be seen.

Instead they moved through the wood at the bottom of the garden, then set off towards what Roberta knew vaguely was another Highway that would eventually lead them to San Francisco.

She would have liked to take the train, but it was obvious that if she and Danny were seen at the station it would cause comment, and the great thing was to disappear without anybody having the slightest idea where they had gone.

She had the feeling that once they had vanished no one would make much effort to find them again.

The Doctor who treated the Minister would know he had died of a heart-attack and would think perhaps that it had been brought on by finding that she and Danny had run away.

There were all sorts of things they could think, but for her the most important aim was to put as many miles as possible between themselves and Blue River before the morning.

Roberta was used to walking, as she had often preferred to walk, in the desert rather than sway about on the camels.

Sometimes her father added horses to their caravan and then she enjoyed riding more than anything else.

But horses were not always available, and in some places it was impossible to keep them well and strong enough to endure the long journeys they had taken.

But she had forgotten how heavy the grip would become or that she had Danny with her, whose legs were small and for whom it was long past his bedtime.

However they reached the Highway in about two hours, then sat down by the roadside hoping it would be possible for them to get a lift.

It was unlikely that anybody from Blue River would pick them up or in any way connect them later with the tragedy of the Minister's death.

They had sat by the roadside for nearly half-an-hour and Danny was almost asleep when a wagon came along.

Roberta waved to him, the driver stopped, and she saw that he was a large man with a strong, nasal accent.

"Wanna lift, Lady?" he enquired.

"Yes, please," Roberta answered.

"Jump up."

She lifted Danny up into the wagon and Columbus sprang up on his own.

She would have put the child between her and the driver, but he said:

"Sit next to me so's I can talk to you. It's lonely driving for miles alone."

Because he was obliging them with a lift Roberta saw no reason why she should not do as he asked.

She therefore settled Danny on the other side of her and put her arm around him to hold him close. Columbus sat on the seat the other side looking out with bright intelligent eyes.

The driver started his horses again, saying as he did so:

"Where are you a–going?"

"To San Francisco eventually," Roberta replied, "but it would be kind of you if you would put us down somewhere where we can have a bed for the night."

"I knows just the place," the man replied, "and they have good hamburgers too!"

"That sounds delightful," Roberta replied, "and thank you very much for stopping. My little boy is very tired."

"He's yours?"

"Yes," Roberta lied, "I am a widow, and I am going to San Francisco to live with my relations."

She thought as she spoke that it was a good thing she had somebody on whom she could try out her story so that she would have it clear in her mind in case she was later asked a lot of questions.

They chatted and the driver told her of the long journeys he took, carrying goods from one town to another, or taking chickens and turkeys from the farmers to the markets.

"It's a living," he said, "but a tiring one."

"And you have no family of your own?"

"Now now," he replied. "M'wife left me with one of m'friends, and I've not set eyes on her for five years!"

"I am sorry," Roberta said sympathetically, "it must be very lonely for you."

"It be that," the driver replied.

The horses plodded on, obviously tired after a long day.

The stars were now bright in the sky, and there was also a rising moon which made everything seem magical and very beautiful.

Roberta was deep in her thoughts when the driver, after a silence that had lasted nearly a quarter-of-an-hour, said:

"I've bin a—thinking. You're a pretty little thing, and as you say, I'm lonely and without your man you must be lonely too."

There was a note in his voice that had not been there before and Roberta stiffened. Then she asked:

"How much further have we got to go?"

"'Bout a mile," the driver said. "If you want to stay the night, you can stay with me. We'll have a bite of supper together and afterwards I'll make up for the death of your hubby, just as you can help me to forget my Nelly — damn her eyes!"

"I think that is something you will never do," Roberta replied.

"You leave it all to me," the driver said putting a hand for a moment on her knee. "The boy and the dog can sleep in the back of the wagon. There's room for them there, and you and me can be real cozy."

The way he spoke and the passion behind his words frightened Roberta.

She was aware, as she had not been before, how completely defenceless she would be against a man as strong as the one sitting beside her, and how difficult it would be to escape from him.

She had a sudden terror that if she did not agree to what he was suggesting he might stop the wagon here and now, and perhaps drag her to the side of the road.

Once again he took his hand from the reins and as he pressed her knee again he said:

"I might have known when I picked you up I was in for a bit o' fun! You're real pretty and I'll tell you how much that means when I see you in less than you're wearing at the moment."

He laughed as if it was a good joke and Roberta felt herself shiver.

Then as she saw the light of an Inn just ahead of them she prayed frantically there would be a way of escape.

"Help me, Papa, help me!" she said in her heart. "I do not know what to do, but you would know, and you must tell me."

"Here we are!" the driver said. "Now just you and the boy go inside, find a table and sit down at it. I'll join you as soon as I've put the horses in the stable, and I'll see about getting a room with a nice big bed for the two of us."

He gave her a nudge with his arm, not seeming to expect a reply.

Danny was asleep and Roberta woke him up.

Carrying her grip and with Columbus at their heels they went into the Inn.

There were a number of wagon-drivers, big and strong men, eating at tables or at the bar which stretched the length of the room.

A man in shirt-sleeves who appeared to be the Proprietor bade them good evening and Roberta asked:

"Could we have a table for three, please? The gentleman I am with is just putting away his wagon."

There was a table at the end of the room and as the man walked ahead of them Roberta added:

"Perhaps first my son and I could wash?"

The man pointed to a door leading off the main room and she hurriedly went through it to find herself in a passageway which seemed to lead to the back of the Inn.

She was not mistaken and a few minutes later they had left the Inn and were hurrying over open ground finding their way by the light of the moon and the stars.

"Where are we going, Aunt Roberta?" Danny asked sleepily.

"Mama—not 'Aunt Roberta!'"

"Mama! Where are we going?"

"I do not know," Roberta replied truthfully, "anywhere away from the Inn!"

"Why? I'se thirsty. I want something to drink."

"We will find something, I am sure we will find something," Roberta said. "But for the moment we just have to get away."

Danny was too sleepy to ask any more questions, but she knew as he dragged on her hand and walked more and more slowly that he was very tired.

Still she urged him on.

"We must find somewhere because Columbus needs a drink," she said. "He must be very thirsty."

"I'se very thirsty," Danny complained. "Very, very thirsty! And hungry too!"

Seeing that he had already had a meal Roberta thought this need could not be very strong.

At the same time, the dust on the road had left her almost as thirsty as he was.

They walked on and on, and she was just beginning to think that she could go no further and they would have to sit down under a tree for the night, when ahead she saw a twinkling light.

"If it is a farmhouse," she reasoned to herself, "I can at least ask them if we can stay in one of their barns, and I am sure they would be kind enough to give us something to drink."

"Look, Danny," she said. "There is a light."

"A long—way," Danny replied. "I'se tired and—Columbus is—tired too."

"Columbus is lucky, he has four legs," Roberta said, "while we have only two."

"If he has—four legs they will—all be tired," Danny said logically.

It was then Roberta realised that beyond the light she could see the sea.

She had vaguely been aware from what she had seen on

the map that in certain places the main road ran close to the sea.

Now she could see the moonlight glinting on the water, and as they grew nearer still she could hear the soft splash of the waves on the shore.

She had a sudden fear that the light she had seen was not that of a house, but perhaps of a beacon or a warning light of some sort.

Then as she walked on, by this time having to drag Danny and finding she was almost exhausted by the heaviness of her grip, she saw in front of her what appeared to be a wooden shack.

There was only one window and a door on this side of it, although she suspected there would be a verandah facing the sea.

She stopped for a moment trying to catch her breath and thinking out what she should say to the occupant.

She was praying it would be somebody kind who would give Danny something to drink and perhaps let them sleep the night on the verandah, if there was nowhere else.

Then she walked resolutely forward pulling Danny with her and put down the grip before she reached out to knock on the door.

Her knock did not sound very loud and after a moment, as there was no reply, she knocked again.

It was then unexpectedly quickly that the door opened and she saw there was a tall man on the other side of it.

"Good evening," Roberta said as he did not speak. "My son and I have . . . lost our way. We wonder if you would be very . . . kind and let us stay here until it is . . . light. We have walked for a long time and we are very tired and thirsty."

Still the man did not speak and Roberta felt despairingly

that perhaps she would be refused and the door would be shut in their faces.

Then in a voice that was quiet, but with a note of amusement in it he said:

"I was certainly not expecting visitors at this hour, but of course come in."

Roberta realised as he spoke that she had been holding her breath.

Now she let it out and stepped over the threshold, seeing that the inside of the house was far larger than she might have expected.

The light from two oil lamps seemed dazzlingly bright after the darkness, and she could see there was a sofa and two comfortable chairs arranged around a large fireplace that was burning logs.

Most surprising of all, there was an easel set up in the centre of the room and around the walls and stacked on the floor were a number of canvases.

Because it was so surprising and so far from what she had expected Roberta exclaimed:

"You are an artist!"

As she spoke she turned back to the man who had closed the door behind them and knew to her astonishment that she had seen him before.

It was the American she had noticed on the train journey from New Orleans, the man who had seemed different from everybody else.

chapter four

FOR a moment Roberta just stared at the man and he stared
at her.

Then without thinking she said the first thing that came
into her mind.

"I saw you on the train from New Orleans!"

He smiled and it made him look even more handsome.

"I had been South to sell a picture, but surely you are
English?"

The way he spoke made Roberta feel that perhaps she
had been indiscreet and quickly she looked away from him,
moving without realising she was doing so, towards the
easel.

Only when she was standing in front of it and she could
see the canvas which was only half-finished she exclaimed:

"But you are an Impressionist!"

In a surprised voice he asked as he crossed the room to
stand beside her:

"What do you know about Impressionists?"

"I have seen their pictures in Paris."

Again she was speaking without thinking and it flashed through her mind that it must seem a very strange thing that here in the middle of nowhere was a young woman who had been to France and who knew anything at all about Impressionist painting.

But it was too late to take back the words she had already spoken and as she saw the surprise and puzzlement in his eyes she said quickly:

"Yes, I am English, but my son has been brought up in America, which is why I have come here."

"Suppose we introduce ourselves?" the man said. "My name is Adam—Adam Fawcett."

"And mine is Roberta Boscombe."

Adam held out his hand.

"I am pleased to meet you, Mrs. Boscombe, and I am delighted to be of service, although it seems mysterious that you should arrive here so late."

"Danny and I lost our way," Roberta replied a little lamely.

As if the sound of his name woke him when he was standing just inside the door half-asleep Danny said:

"I'se tired and I'se thirsty, and so's Columbus!"

"As if his voice made Adam aware of him for the first time he stopped looking at Roberta and said:

"Then we must certainly do something about that! Come into the kitchen where I'll get a bowl for the dog and some lemonade which will quench your thirst."

He went to the side of the big room as he spoke and opened a door through which Roberta had a glimpse of a small kitchen.

While Danny and Columbus followed Adam she remained behind, looking around the room which she realised made an excellent Studio with several large windows overlooking the sea.

The curtains were undrawn and she could see the moonlight on the water and thought it was a perfect place for an artist.

Then she looked again at the canvas on the easel and was aware that he painted well, and very much in the style of the Impressionists whose pictures she had seen in Paris.

Her father had told her how controversial they were and how the critics laughed derisively at them.

"At the same time," the Earl had said, "I think they have something which is often lacking in the work of other artists."

"What is that?" Roberta had asked.

"Light," her father replied, "the light which makes the Impressionists see everything in a different way from any other artist in the past."

Because Roberta had been genuinely interested and he thought it educational for her, he had taken her to some of the Exhibitions in Montmartre and other parts of Paris where the Impressionists were showing their pictures.

Some she found incomprehensible, some were definitely very beautiful, but what they all had was a new portrayal of the play of light in nature, a light which afterwards she thought she found in the desert.

It had made their paintings unique, quite different from the older Masters who relied on academic techniques which had long been accepted as correct.

She could understand why the Impressionists appealed so strongly to her father who was so rebellious against anything conventional and conservative.

He had brought two or three of the pictures he admired and which when they left for Africa had been stored with a lot of their other belongings in Paris.

Roberta knew they now belonged to her, and she thought that when she could have a house of her own she would send for them and be proud to hang them on her walls, however much other people might criticise them in a derogatory manner.

All these ideas were flashing through her mind, when she heard Adam call from the kitchen:

"I have some coffee for you, Mrs. Boscombe, and as your son says he is hungry, perhaps you are hungry too."

As she had had nothing to eat before they left Blue River Roberta replied:

"I would like that. I am hungry despite being so tired."

"You must tell me where you have come from, and why you are here," Adam said.

He pulled a chair out from the table as he spoke, and she sat down, thinking the kitchen was very bare and she was quite certain that if he was looking after himself he seldom troubled to cook anything.

As if he read her thoughts he said:

"As I am alone here, when it grows too dark to paint, I usually walk down to the Drugstore and get myself a hamburger. Otherwise if I am hungry, I have a few slices of ham."

"I do not call that a proper diet for a growing man!" Roberta remarked.

He laughed.

"I manage well on it. But your son looks as if he needs feeding."

"Yes, I know," Roberta said quickly, "and that is why I have taken him away from where he has been staying and we are going to San Francisco."

"Have you been there before?"

She shook her head.

Then because she was frightened of having questions put to her that she could not answer she said:

"Tell me why you are an Impressionist. It is certainly

something I did not expect to find here in America."

"It is the way I have always wanted to paint," Adam replied. "I thought it was my own original idea until I saw the Impressionists in Paris."

"You have been to Paris?" Roberta exclaimed.

She suddenly thought how exciting it would be to talk with somebody who had perhaps seen the same Exhibitions as she had herself.

Then even as the words came to her lips she realised that Danny was falling asleep at the other end of the table.

"I am afraid we are imposing on you," she said in a low voice, "but is there somewhere where we could spend the night? We are not particular, and if there is nowhere else I am sure we could manage on the floor."

"I would not be so inhospitable as not to offer you my own bed," Adam replied, "except that it is unnecessary. This place is bigger than you might think."

As he spoke he picked Danny up in his arms and carried him back through the main room to the other side of it.

Roberta saw there were two doors, one of which was ajar and she could see that it was his room.

The other door led into quite a small bedroom but there was a bed against one wall and a couch against the other.

"When it is warm enough," Adam said, "I sleep on the verandah, but the nights are still cool enough for me to prefer being inside."

As he spoke he put Danny gently down on the couch, putting a cushion behind his head.

Then going to a chest-of-drawers which was the only other furniture in the room he opened a drawer and pulled out a woollen blanket.

"I think this should keep him warm enough," he said.

"I am sure it will," Roberta replied. "Thank you very much."

"Now may I suggest," Adam said, "that you undress him and put him to bed, then come and tell me a little about yourself. In the meantime, I will brew up some more coffee. I think there are some eggs in the kitchen, if you would like them with cold ham."

"I would enjoy the eggs," Roberta replied, "but, please, let me cook them myself. I am a very good cook."

Adam smiled.

"That is the best news I have had for a long time! I would like to add that the hamburger I had earlier this evening was not very palatable."

Roberta laughed as he went out of the room closing the door behind him.

It did not take her long to undress Danny, who was so soundly asleep that he had no idea what was happening to him.

She put on his flannel nightshirt, covered him with the blanket and knew it was unlikely that he would move until the morning.

She had taken off her bonnet and now she saw there was a mirror over the chest and she untied her hair in it.

"We are very lucky to find somewhere to sleep tonight," she told her reflection.

She knew too she felt an excitement at having met again the man she had noticed on the train journey and had wondered if it was possible to speak to him.

She thought of how fortunate she had been to escape from the ardent wagon-driver and was quite certain her father had been looking after her and protecting her.

"Thank you, Papa," she said softly.

There was a smile on her lips as she opened the door and went back towards the kitchen.

*   *   *

After she had made an omelette with the eggs and found several pieces of ham to go with it Adam sat back in his chair and said:

"I enjoyed that! You are quite right, you are a good cook!"

"If you are living here alone why do you not find somebody to look after you?" Roberta enquired, thinking of Mrs. Ski and how capable she had been.

"I do not want women messing about the place," Adam replied, "and I cannot always afford it."

She looked at him in surprise, thinking that the house, although it was roughly built, was comfortably equipped, and while Adam was casually dressed he did not look at all poor.

"I have to live on what I can make from my pictures," he explained. "When I sell one I am rich, but when there are no buyers I am hungry. It is as simple as that!"

"Are there many buyers of Impressionist art in America?" Roberta asked.

She remembered how her father had said that nobody would buy Impressionists in Paris with the result that those he had bought had been absurdly cheap.

Adam laughed.

"That is obviously a question I have no wish to answer," he said, "but if you want the truth, when I am nearly down to bedrock I have to paint something which is saleable, although I feel like a traitor in doing so."

"I think it is sensible of you," Roberta replied, "for after all you have to live!"

He pushed his plate away, put his arms on the table and said:

"Now, tell me about yourself."

To her own surprise Roberta had an impulse to tell him the truth.

Then she knew it would be a very stupid thing to do, for she knew nothing about this man who might easily talk about her when she had gone, and then the authorities, although she was not certain who they were, would take Danny away from her.

Instead she said in a low voice:

"My husband is dead and Danny and I are going to San Francisco for the time being, at any rate."

"Was your husband English?"

Roberta thought for a moment. Then she said quickly:

"No, American."

"Then I think you should bring up your son as an American," Adam said. "He is a very good-looking little boy."

"Thank you," Roberta answered.

"It is not surprising," Adam went on, "considering how beautiful you are, but I expect a great many men have told you that."

Roberta wanted to laugh, knowing that in the last two years when she had been with her father and Francine in the desert there had been nobody but the camel-boys and the camels to admire her.

As she did not speak after a moment Adam went on:

"I want to paint you, although God knows if I can do you justice."

"I thought you would prefer landscapes," Roberta replied, because she felt she must say something.

"I do," Adam admitted, "but you are different!"

He sat looking at her and she felt the colour rise in her cheeks.

"You are very lovely!" he said, after a moment as if he spoke to himself.

"You are making me embarrassed," she protested.

As she spoke it occurred to her that if she really were

the married woman she pretended to be, she would not be shy and would not blush.

But there was nothing she could do about it, and she only hoped the man opposite her would not think it strange.

"How long will you be staying?" he asked.

Roberta was about to say that she and Danny must leave the next day, then as her eyes met Adam's across the table it was somehow impossible to say anything but only to be held captive in a way she did not understand.

"Please stay," he said after a moment. "I want you to. Besides, the boy is tired and he would enjoy playing on the sands and bathing in the sea."

This was indisputably true, but Roberta thought if she was sensible she would go away.

Then she knew that every instinct in her body was telling her to stay where she was, where if she did so, she would be safe.

When she thought about it, it was very frightening to envisage what she should do when she reached San Francisco, alone without knowing one soul in the City, or having any idea where they could stay.

It flashed through her mind that there might be other men like the wagon-driver and perhaps the next time it might not be so easy to escape.

As she thought of how she had managed to evade him and remembered the long, tiring walk they had had before reaching their present refuge, and above all the shock of the Minister's death, the whole horror of what had happened so quickly swept over her like a tidal wave.

In a voice that did not sound like her own, she said:

"Perhaps we could . . . stay for a . . . few days."

"That is what I wanted you to say," Adam answered.

She remembered how poor he had said he was and added quickly:

"We can pay for our board and lodging."

"Are you insulting me?"

"No, of course not."

"I have sold three pictures in Los Angeles, so at the moment I am rich!"

"I have no wish to impose on you."

"You will not do that, and I shall expect you to sit for me and also to do the cooking!"

She laughed, and he raised his eye-brows to ask:

"Why are you laughing?"

In fact, it was amusing Roberta that it seemed that wherever she went her cooking came in useful. But she replied:

"I think I was just feeling happy to be here and not have to worry about moving on tomorrow. I have not been in America before, and I find it very large and rather bewildering."

"Then you married your husband when he was in Europe!"

Too late Roberta remembered she had been speaking as herself and not as Mrs. Boscombe.

"Yes," she said quickly, "and a relative of my husband took Danny to live with them until we could come out here."

"But your husband died before he could do so," Adam said, as if he was working it out.

Roberta felt as if she was sinking deeper and deeper into a pit she had dug for herself.

She got up from the table.

"I will wash up the plates," she said, "then as I am very tired, I would like to go to bed."

"As you are very tired," Adam replied, "I will wash them for you."

"Why not leave them until the morning?"

"I am sure that is a very slovenly thing to do," he replied mockingly, "but if you insist, I agree."

They both laughed as if it sounded very funny.

As Roberta reached her bedroom and shut the door behind her she knew that in some way she did not understand she was happy for the first time since her father had been taken ill.

She had laughed as she used to laugh with him. Although there was little physical resemblance between them, Adam made her feel as if she was with her father again.

It was the same feeling as being protected and being looked after, and his blue eyes twinkled in the same way that her father's had done.

"I am lucky, so very lucky!" she said to herself.

Then as Columbus lay down beside Danny's couch she undressed and slipped into the bed, finding that although it was narrow it was surprisingly comfortable.

Before she could even begin to say the prayers she had always said at night, she was asleep.

* * *

Roberta awoke, coming back to reality through clouds of sleep.

As she did so, she heard the bedroom door click and knew that Danny had just crept out having dressed himself without waking her.

She heard him in the Sitting-Room talking, and Adam's deep voice replying.

Then as she told herself she must get up and cook the breakfast, she knew from the way their voices faded away into the distance that they had gone out onto the beach.

Slowly, because it was an effort to move, she sat up and looked around the very small bedroom thinking she had hardly taken it in last night.

Now she was aware that sparsely furnished as it was,

there were thick rugs on the floor, and the curtains shutting out the sunshine were prettily patterned with flowers in bright colours.

She felt a new energy sweep through her and she jumped out of bed and washed herself in the cold water in the basin that stood in one corner of the room.

She twisted her hair into a chignon, pinning it tightly to her head without worrying particularly how it looked, put on one of the light muslin gowns she had packed in her grip and hurried into the Sitting-Room.

As she guessed, the door in the centre of it opened out onto a verandah and she could see Adam and Danny down by the sea.

They were throwing a stick into the waves and Columbus was jumping in after it to bring it back to them.

She went into the kitchen feeling she must pay for her night's rest by starting work immediately.

She found to her relief that despite the number of eggs she had used last night in making the omelette for herself and Adam, there were still enough left for breakfast.

She would have liked to cook something more original than scrambled eggs, but Adam had spoken the truth when he said he did not bother to cook for himself.

The cupboard which acted as a larder appeared to be empty of everything except salt and pepper, a loaf of stale bread and some butter.

She found that Adam had a good fire going in the kitchen stove, so she toasted the bread, spread it with butter, and with the scrambled eggs on top of it, it looked quite appetising. Then she went onto the verandah to call out that breakfast was ready.

Adam, Danny and a very wet Columbus came hurrying back to her.

She noticed with a sense of relief that Adam did not seem

to mind when the dog shook himself then sat on the floor leaving a wet patch from his ragged coat.

She gave Adam and Danny the scrambled eggs, and they ate them in silence, until Adam said:

"You must forgive me if I omitted because of the delicious food you have cooked, to tell you how lovely you look this morning. Are you ready to sit for me?"

"Certainly not!" Roberta replied firmly. "The first thing we have to do is find something substantial for luncheon."

She thought he looked disappointed and she added:

"If you want to paint I will go to the shops, but you must tell me where they are."

"I will go. I think you walked far enough last night and you should now sit on the verandah and behave like a Lady of Leisure, at least until I return."

"Can I take Columbus down to the sea?" Danny asked.

"Yes, of course you can," Roberta replied, "but keep in front of the house where I can see you."

"Columbus likes swimming in the sea, and I want to swim too."

"I will teach you," Adam said. "Have you a bathing-suit?"

Danny shook his head.

"Then I will buy one for you, and one for your mother."

Before Roberta could say anything he exclaimed:

"That is an idea! I will paint you as a mermaid coming out of the sea, or perhaps a Siren would be a better description, like those who tried to entice Ulysses!"

"I am not certain, remembering how he stuffed the ears of his crew with wax to prevent them from hearing their cries, and had himself roped to the mast, that that is a compliment!"

"If you want compliments," Adam said, "I will have to brush up on my vocabulary."

"I would not like to put you to any trouble."

She knew his eyes were twinkling as he answered:

"May I say it would be a pleasure, Mrs. Boscombe?"

He was teasing her and she laughed.

It was something she had never been able to do before with any man except her father, and she wondered if he had any idea how inexperienced she was and how ignorant of how to be light-hearted with a man who was more or less her own age.

She had watched women flirting with her father, enticing him with every possible wile, with their eyes, their lips, their hands, and the sinuous movements of their bodies.

Where Francine was concerned it had been an exotic performance which might have taken place on the stage.

But none of it was the same as what was a kind of fencing with words which had other and half-concealed meanings behind them.

"What do you want me to buy?" Adam asked.

"Shall I make a list?"

"It is something you had better do, for I refuse categorically to return for anything I have forgotten!"

She laughed and he went on:

"Quite frankly it is a waste of time and sunlight to fuss about food, when I might be painting."

"As long as I am the cook," Roberta said, "I have no intention of allowing either you or Danny to go hungry, and Columbus expects at least one very large meal every day!"

"I will bring back enough food to last for a week!"

Roberta gave a cry of horror.

"It would go bad in this heat!" she exclaimed. Besides as I have every intention of varying the menu, I shall insist on having something different every day."

"You are bullying me," Adam protested, "and that is

exactly why I have managed up until now to keep alive without any feminine assistance."

"Is that a tactful way of suggesting that we have outstayed our welcome?" Roberta enquired.

She knew as she spoke that he had no wish for her to leave, but she wanted to make him say so.

He walked away from her. Then in a quiet voice he said:

"If you vanish while I am away, I swear I will catch up with you and bring you back. So just stay here until I return."

She wanted to answer him provocatively, wanted to make him apprehensive that she might in fact, go when he least expected it.

But he turned round and as their eyes met she found that everything flew out of her head.

All she could think of was that his eyes were very blue and there was something magnetic about him which made her feel as if he was drawing her nearer and nearer to him and there was no escape.

Then almost abruptly he walked away and she saw him striding across the rough land and under the trees to where somewhere on the main highway she knew there were a few shops where he bought his food.

She made her own bed, then Danny's and after a moment's hesitation went into Adam's room.

She expected it to be very untidy, but surprisingly his clothes were neatly put away behind a curtain, and there was little lying about.

She made his bed which like her own, looked very comfortable, but was much larger. Then she noticed for the first time that facing it on the wall was an Impressionist picture.

She thought it was by Monet or Sisley, she was not sure which, but it was very beautiful.

She stood looking at it for a long time, feeling as if the light in it was something she had always wanted to find, but had never understood until now how beautiful it could be.

Then, as if she must compare it with Adam's, she went into the Sitting-Room to look at the pictures stacked against the wall.

Some were finished, some were only just begun, then had been discarded.

She felt sure that Adam had a touch of genius in his painting because his method was revolutionary.

But Impressionism was, she knew, unappreciated and roundly denounced by those who admired the traditional techniques of portraying what they saw.

She only wished her father was with her, to tell her what he thought of Adam's paintings.

Her instinct, however, told her that Adam was good. At least, if not yet very experienced, going in the right direction so that perhaps one day he would be acclaimed.

'I hope so, I do hope so!' she thought fervently, but did not ask herself why it mattered so much.

She had joined Danny at the edge of the sea when a long time later Adam came back.

Having removed her shoes and stockings so that she could walk comfortably on the sand, she was standing a little way into the water, holding up her skirts to avoid getting them wet, when she heard his voice behind her.

"I am back," he called, "and I have brought you a mountain of food!"

She turned round to look at him and he exclaimed:

"That is how I should paint you! God, if I could only get it down on canvas!"

She walked out of the water towards him and he said:

"Do not move! Stay where you are!"

Roberta laughed at him.

"The water is too cold for my feet," she said. "Besides

I want to go and see what you have brought me from the stores."

"Food! Food!" Adam exclaimed. "Do you never think of anything else?"

"You will be thinking about it in an hour's time!" Roberta retorted.

Despite Adam's protests she walked back towards the house.

"I took so long," he said, "because I bought both you and Danny bathing-suits. Yours is very glamorous, and will attract any man who might be watching you."

Roberta looked up and down the deserted beach.

"Where are they?" she asked. "There is so little sign of human beings that we might be in the desert."

"Are you telling me," Adam asked, "that you have been in the desert, or was that just a figure of speech?"

"Think what you like," Roberta answered. "It will give you something to ponder on."

"Why should you be so mysterious?" he enquired.

"I am not!" she protested.

She knew as she spoke that it was not really because she was being mysterious but because in some strange way Adam could read her thoughts that his intuition told him that when she mentioned the desert it was because she had actually been there.

"I must be careful," she warned herself.

Then she knew that was something she somehow could not be when she and Adam were together.

*　　*　　*

Roberta cooked them a large luncheon, thinking it best for Danny's sake for them to have a light meal in the evening.

It was easy to be proficient on the oil-stove which she was sure was both expensive and up-to-date.

It certainly enabled her to produce food which made man, boy and dog enjoy every mouthful.

"You are Wonder Woman!" Adam said as he finished. "In fact, I do not think you are real at all, but sent by the gods to help me when I most needed it."

"I want to swim in the sea," Danny said as soon as he had finished.

"Not for at least an hour after a meal," Roberta replied. "But you can put on your swimming-suit which kind Mr. Adam has bought for you."

"*Uncle* Adam!" Danny corrected. "I like him, so I've made him my uncle."

"And I like you!" Adam said. "So I am going to turn you into a small fish and you will be able to swim far better than they do!"

Danny exclaimed with delight and ran into the bedroom to change.

Only when he and Adam had gone to the beach did Roberta do the same.

She felt a little shy, although she had often swum in Africa when they camped near a like or a river.

Her father and Francine had swum too and she had never given a thought to the fact that she was wearing very few clothes and that no English Ladies swam, however hot the summer might be.

She was aware it was something that would horrify her grandmother and that Aunt Emily would add it to the list of sins they had compiled against her father.

The swimming-suit Adam had bought her was made of a cheap material and she suspected it was only the poorest and least respectable girls along the coast who dared to bathe in the sea.

It was nevertheless attractive. The colour made her skin seem very white, and while the costume revealed her legs it had a skirt and sleeves that reached a little above the elbows of her bare arms.

Yet somehow she felt naked as she walked down the steps of the verandah and over the rough ground which led onto the golden sand of the beach.

Danny saw her first and ran out of the water to say:

"Come and watch me swim! I can swim a little way by myself."

"That is very clever of you!" Roberta smiled.

"Is Uncle Adam going to teach you to swim too?" Danny asked.

"There is no need for him to do that," Roberta replied, "for I can swim already!"

She saw Adam coming towards her and ran into the water to strike out, hoping it would surprise him.

Only a few seconds later, when he was swimming beside her did she realise she had succeeded.

"Where did you learn to swim like that?" he asked. "As it could not have been in Paris, I imagine it must have been the desert of which you spoke so confidently just now."

She did not reply and after a moment he said:

"I suppose you know you are driving me mad with curiosity?"

"I cannot think why you are so interested!"

"That is something I will explain to you a little later, but now, unless you want Danny to drown himself by trying to follow us, I think I had better go back."

He turned round as he spoke and because Roberta could not help it, she followed him.

*   *   *

Roberta sat on the verandah with Adam, watching the stars coming out in the sky.

An exhausted Danny had been put to bed immediately after supper, and as Roberta kissed him good-night he said:

"It's been a very exciting day, Aunt Roberta!"

"Mama!" she corrected.

"Mama," he murmured sleepily, "and tomorrow will be— exciting too."

"Yes, I'm sure it will," she agreed. "Now go to sleep. You must be very tired after being so long in the water."

"It was *gorgeous.*"

Robert knew this was a word he had picked up from Adam, and in a sleepy voice he added:

"Columbus thought it—*gorgeous* too!"

When Roberta had joined Adam on the verandah she said:

"Danny says it has been a *gorgeous* day. I have never heard him use that word until now."

"It is something you taught me," Adam explained. "You are a gorgeous girl, who cooks gorgeous food, and it is a perfect word to describe somebody who is beautiful and generous and full of laughter."

"Then I am very glad to be 'gorgeous!'" Roberta laughed. "But I have never thought of myself like that before."

"There are a great many other ways of describing you," Adam said. "Tomorrow I intend to start my picture and nothing you can say or do is going to stop me."

"I did not deliberately stop you today."

"You know I could not paint because I could not bear to leave you and Danny by the sea."

The way he spoke gave her a strange feeling she had never known before.

Because she was a little afraid of it, she said:

"It has been a gorgeous day but, like Danny, I am very tired."

"Then you must go to bed," Adam said. "And thank you, Roberta, for making us all so happy."

Roberta had risen to her feet and now she raised her face to ask ingenuously:

"Have I really done that?"

It was a childish question because she wanted to be re-assured.

She was standing near the edge of the verandah and the moonlight was on her face and turning her golden hair to silver.

As he was so tall Adam was in the shadow of the roof.

She strained her eyes trying to see the expression on his face. Then he said in a voice she did not recognise:

"How can I answer that question in words?"

He put his arms round her and pulled her against him as he spoke.

Then to her surprise because she had not anticipated it, his lips came down on hers.

Roberta had never been kissed before and as his mouth held her captive she thought she should push him away, but somehow it was impossible.

Then when she tried to think, everything was swept from her mind except for the strange feeling that seemed to move through her body and into her lips.

It was as if the moonlight was not only outside but inside, and she could feel its rays flickering through her until it was impossible to think, but only to feel that she was no longer herself, but part of Adam.

His lips were at first gentle and compelling.

Then as he drew her closer still they became demanding, possessive and something she had never known before, passionate.

He kissed her until she felt as if her feet were no longer on the ground and she was floating in the sky amongst the stars.

The moonlight was shining through them both and their bodies pulsated with it.

She could feel his heart beating against hers and she knew this was a wonder and a beauty above anything she had ever known or imagined.

Then as Adam raised his head she suddenly remembered that he was a man she had met only yesterday, and that if anybody knew that she was being kissed in such a manner they would be shocked and horrified by her behaviour.

With a little cry that had something childlike about it, she pulled herself free of his arms.

Swiftly, before he could stop her, she sped from the verandah into the Sitting-Room and from there into her own bedroom.

Only as she shut the door behind her did she feel as if her heart was beating so tumultuously that it might burst from her breast, and her breath was coming in little gasps from between her lips.

At the same time, the whole world was filled with a glory that was indescribable.

She knew that when Adam had kissed her she had touched the stars and never again would be content with the earth as she had known it until now.

"This is . . . love," she whispered to herself.

Then she was afraid because it was so very different from what she had expected.

chapter five

ADAM was painting Roberta, but not by the sea, as she had expected. Instead he had made her sit beyond the house under one of the trees which was in blossom.

Because the soil in California was so rich, the wild grass was filled with flowers, and in her white muslin gown she looked like a flower herself as the sunshine percolated through the branches above her and turned her hair to gold.

He set up the easel and sat on a stool concentrating fiercely on his canvas.

Roberta had not dared to look at him when she went into the kitchen to cook the breakfast and, although they talked in front of Danny of ordinary things, it seemed as though every word they spoke had a different meaning from what they actually said.

"I am going to paint you this morning," Adam said, "and I want no arguments about it."

"Very well," Roberta replied, "but if you are hungry by luncheon-time, do not blame me."

Adam did not answer.

He merely began to collect his things from the Sitting-Room, and because Roberta knew it would irritate him if she delayed she just stacked the plates in the sink and hurried out into the sunshine.

By this time he was half-way towards the place where he wanted her to sit.

Walking behind him she saw how tall and broad-shouldered he was, and how he walked with a grace which was surprisingly in so large a man.

After he had begun to paint and the sun grew a little hotter, he pulled off his shirt impatiently as if it was restricting him.

It was then, looking at him from where she was sitting, that Roberta felt shy.

Yesterday when they had been swimming and he had only worn swimming trunks, she had not thought it at all strange that he should be naked above the waist.

She had been so used to seeing the natives of Africa with very little on that nakedness meant little to her, and certainly it did not shock her as it would have any other English girl who had not travelled as she had.

Now, because she was in love, she could not help thinking how beautiful Adam's body was with his spare shoulders and narrow hips.

It seemed to her that he was perfectly proportioned like one of Michaelangelo's statues which she had seen in Rome.

It made her blush to think he had held her close to him and kissed her last night and how wonderful it had been.

'I love him,' she thought, 'but I am sure I mean nothing to him!'

Although she knew something about love because of her father's many affairs, she had been too young to have anything to do with the flirtatious Frenchmen before leaving France.

Roberta was therefore completely un-self-conscious and unawakened where men were concerned.

Now, as she looked at Adam painting her, she wanted to be in his arms again and to feel his lips on hers.

Then she thought of her grandmother and knew how horrified she would be if she knew where she was at the moment, and what she was doing and thinking.

It suddenly struck Roberta that it was very reprehensible that she was staying unchaperoned in a man's house and that she was looking at him half-naked and he had seen her swimming in the sea.

"It is different away from England," she excused herself.

At the same time, she had a feeling of guilt which was uncomfortable.

Danny was playing with Columbus at the edge of the water, and she could hear his voice talking to the dog.

The only other sound was the song of the birds in the trees, and the murmur of the sea.

'I am happy,' Roberta thought. 'I have never been so happy.'

She knew her happiness was centred on the man who was trying to portray her on canvas.

She must have sat for two hours before he rose from his stool, stood back to look at the canvas on the easel, and walked towards her.

"You have been very good," he said, "and I have done a lot of work. Now I feel it is a waste of time to be painting when I might be kissing you."

The way he spoke was a surprise and when he sat down beside her she instinctively put up her hands to ward him off.

"How . . . far have you . . . got with my portrait?" she asked and knew her voice trembled.

"Not far enough," he replied. "Just as it is impossible to

capture the sunlight, so I cannot capture your beauty."

He took her hand in his as he spoke and raised it to his lips.

He kissed her fingers one by one, then turned her hand over to kiss her palm, a long, lingering kiss which made her quiver.

Then he looked into her eyes and said:

"I love you, and I think, my lovely one, you love me just a little."

"It is . . . too soon," Roberta faltered. "We have only . . . just met each . . . other."

"That is not true. We are in love, and it is as if we have known each other for thousands of years and I found you again when I least expected it."

"I think . . . actually . . . I found you!"

"When I saw you standing in the doorway," Adam went on, "the light was on your face, and I thought I must be dreaming."

His fingers tightened on hers.

"I knew you had come to me across time and space and you were what I have always been waiting for."

There was a deep note in his voice which told her he was sincere.

Then as he put his arm around her her head fell naturally against his shoulder.

He kissed her forehead before he said:

"We are going to be very happy, my precious. I think it should be warm enough tonight for Danny to sleep on the verandah, or as my bed is actually bigger than yours, perhaps you should come to me."

For a moment Roberta did not understand what he was saying. Then she stiffened.

"I . . . I do not . . . know what you . . . mean."

"Why pretend?" Adam asked. "We love each other and

the facts have decreed that you should be mine. What happens tomorrow, the day after, or the day after that is immaterial, except that I have no wish, my beautiful, to wait any longer for you."

Before Roberta could reply he put his hand under her chin, turned her face up to his, and his lips were on hers.

He kissed her demandingly, possessively, as if he was convincing her without words that she belonged to him.

She found herself pulsating with the same rapture that he had given her last night.

Again it was impossible to think, but only to feel sensations she had no idea existed and which seeped through her body and made her feel as if she was a part of everything that lived and breathed.

He raised his head and said:

"You have bewitched me, and I am going to find it very hard to wait until tonight."

"You must not... I cannot... I cannot do what you are... saying!" Roberta stammered.

He kissed the tip of her nose, smiled as if he thought what she was saying was nonsense, and getting to his feet walked towards his easel.

Slowly Roberta followed him.

"I must... go and... cook the luncheon," she said in a voice that did not sound like her own.

Then as she reached his side she looked down at what he had painted and saw it was what she had expected, but even better and lovelier.

It was very impressionistic and she was part of the sunshine coming through the branches of the trees. Half her body seemed to have no form of its own, but was merged with the flowers, the trees and the background.

Only her eyes and her mouth were positive and individualistic, and Roberta thought that the painting made her look far more beautiful than she could ever really be.

"What do you think of it?" Adam asked.

"It is . . . wonderful!"

"Do you mean that?"

"I only wish my father could see it! I know he would appreciate your work and say that you were going to be a famous artist."

"That is what I want to be," Adam said. "I *have* to prove myself."

He said the last words as if it was a vow, that somehow he would achieve what he was seeking, however many obstacles there might be in his way.

As if he suddenly realised she was beside him he said:

"Go back! I have a great deal more to do to your face, and your hair is wrong."

"Before you do any more you must eat," Roberta insisted, "and if you are not hungry, I am quite certain Danny will be!"

"You are bullying me!" Adam complained.

"You said you disliked women messing you about," Roberta replied. "So if you do not want us, we can always leave after luncheon."

"Now you are definitely blackmailing me!" Adam said. "What are you? An angel disguised as a cook, or a fantasy of my mind which has no real existence?"

Roberta walked away from him and said over her shoulder:

"I am a cook, housekeeper and nursemaid, and I will call you when luncheon is ready!"

He stood looking at her and she had the feeling he was debating whether he should run after her, pick her up in his arms, and make her obey him.

Then with a little sigh he sat down again at his easel.

Roberta had already planned they would have a cold luncheon, but there was the chicken to be cut up, the mayonnaise to be made, a salad to be tossed in a wooden bowl.

Then there was fruit to be pooled and covered with a sweet syrup.

When it was ready, she took it all out onto the verandah, and when she called Danny came running up from the sea, Columbus beside him.

A few minutes later Adam walked reluctantly away from his easel.

As they ate they laughed and talked. It was only when Roberta's eyes met Adam's that what she was saying flew out of her mind, and there would be a sudden silence in which she felt as if her heart spoke to his.

"*I* want to swim when I've finished," Danny announced.

"And so do I," Roberta said firmly.

"Very well," Adam agreed, "but you have to promise to give me at least two hours later in the afternoon."

"Unless I prefer to rest," Roberta said provocatively.

"Then I will rest with you."

Realising that would be a mistake she said quickly:

"No, I will sit for you. After all, Danny and I must not interrupt your work."

"You have done that already," Adam said. "I thought until you came that it was the most important thing in my life. Now I know I was mistaken!"

The way he spoke made Roberta blush.

Danny however paid no attention to them and jumped up from the table.

"I'm going to put on my swimming-suit," he said. "Will you give me another swimming lesson, Uncle Adam?"

There was a little pause as if Adam had to think about what Danny had said to him before he replied:

"Yes, of course, but we have to wait, as your mother has said, for an hour, otherwise we will all have tummy-ache."

"Then I'll build a big sand-castle," Danny said and ran off to his bedroom to change.

"I think I too will go for a swim," Adam said quietly.

"The exercise will be good for you," Roberta replied.

Because he was looking at her in a way that made her feel shy she went on:

"You will grow fat if you just sit about all day, and I am sure before we came you used to swim a long way out to sea. I have always been told that swimming exercises all the muscles."

There was silence. Then Adam said:

"I adore you! I love everything about you, but there is one thing I do not understand."

"What is that?" Roberta asked.

"How you can look so absurdly young. You must be twenty-five for Danny to be your son, and yet you look and behave like a young girl who has just emerged from the School-Room to find the world a very strange and bewildering place."

"I . . . I am older than I . . . look!"

"Obviously!" Adam agreed. "At the same time, women will think you have found the secret of eternal youth which they have sought since the beginning of time!"

"You are very complimentary."

"I am simply in love! And I find it incredible that it has happened to me so quickly!"

"What you are saying is that in your numerous other love-affairs it has taken a little longer than an hour or so before you said all those pretty things to whoever has taken your fancy!" Roberta teased.

She gave a sudden cry because Adam stood up and swept

her off her feet and into his arms so roughly that it hurt her.

"Do you really believe I have ever loved anybody before in the way I love you?" he asked.

He did not wait for her answer. His mouth held her captive and he kissed her until she was breathless.

Then as they heard Danny coming back through the Sitting-Room they moved apart.

Because of the emotions he had aroused in her Roberta felt unsteady on her feet.

"Please come with me, Uncle Adam!" Danny pleaded. "I'm sure it's time for us to swim."

For a moment Adam hesitated.

Then he walked with the small boy down the steps of the verandah and they set off hand in hand in the direction of the beach.

Roberta watched them go, then sitting down she wondered frantically what she could do about Adam.

She might be innocent, but she was well aware how much she excited him and she knew because he excited her that it was going to be very difficult to resist him.

"He thinks I have been a married woman," she reasoned, "and therefore would not be so shocked at what he is suggesting as a girl would be."

Because her cheeks were glowing and her heart was beating tumultuously it was difficult to think . . .

She wondered whether it would be best for her to tell him the truth about herself, then knew it could be dangerous for Danny.

However kind and loving Adam might be, she knew nothing about him, and as an American he might argue that it was completely wrong for an American boy to be brought up in England.

She tried to think of what her father would have felt if the same thing happened to him but her brain would not function and all she could think of was Adam's lips on hers and the strength of his arms.

"I love him! I love him!" she told herself, but that was no answer to the problem.

She swam with Adam and Danny in the sea. Then as she had promised, she put on her white muslin gown and sat again under the tree.

"Now the light is different from what it was this morning," Adam grumbled, "and because you look even lovelier than you did a few hours ago, I want to start all over again!"

Roberta gave a cry of protest.

"You cannot do that! Finish this picture because I like it, and I am sure it is one of the best you have ever done!"

"Of course it is!" Adam answered. "It is painted with love, and the love that inspired the great artists, the great composers and the great sculptors all through the centuries!"

"Perhaps I shall hang in the Royal Academy, and be very proud."

He laughed.

"That is extremely unlikely! Can you see the Royal Academy, or the Salon for that matter, accepting an Impressionist, and an American at that?"

"Then I will hang it on the wall of my bedroom and look at it every day," Roberta said unthinkingly.

"*We* will look at it!" Adam corrected.

She felt the colour rise in her cheeks and wondered if this was the moment when she should tell him she was not the widow he imagined, but somebody with very little experience who was both shocked and frightened by what he was suggesting.

Then her eyes went to Danny who had returned to his sand-castle on the beach and she knew she dare not take risks with him.

"What can I do? What can I do?" she asked.

She was repeating the same question in her mind when the sun began to lose its heat and she started to cook the supper.

"I am very hungry, Mama!" Danny called from the Sitting-Room.

"You are eating me out of house and home, young man!" she heard Adam say.

It made her realise that they were, in fact, spending quite a lot of Adam's money.

Since he had insisted on buying the food for her, she had not been to the shops, but she was aware that the excellent meat he brought back was not cheap.

She was sure however, that the fruit and vegetables cost very little.

Yet because she wanted to feed Danny well, she had put down on her shopping-list meat, chicken and fish, all of which for three people could come to quite a considerable sum.

'I must offer to pay for our food,' Roberta thought, 'or else I must go to the shops and pay for it myself, as I managed to do when we were in Blue River.'

At the same time she wondered, because Adam was so insistent that she should not tire herself by going shopping, whether in fact he did not want his neighbours to be aware that he had a woman and a child staying with him.

'Perhaps he is ashamed that I am here unchaperoned,' she thought.

It made her feel more guilty than she was feeling already.

The supper was delicious, and by the time it was over Danny was yawning.

"Go to bed, darling," Roberta said. "I will come in a moment to kiss you goodnight."

"Uncle Adam said I could sleep on the verandah," Danny said. "I'd like that."

"I think it is still too chilly at night for you to be out-of-doors," Roberta said firmly.

She looked at Adam defiantly as she spoke, and he smiled as if he knew she was trying to give him her answer through the child.

"Good-night, Uncle Adam!"

Danny put his arms around Adam's neck where he was sitting at the table and kissed his cheek.

Then with Columbus following him he ran into the bed-room.

"So you have chosen to come to me!" Adam said softly.

Roberta did not pretend to misunderstand what he was saying.

"I am telling you 'No.' It is something I cannot do."

"Why not, my precious?" he asked. "What is the point of mourning your husband, if that is what you are doing? And quite frankly, I do not believe you loved him very much, or that he taught you anything about love."

Because she felt he was being uncomfortably perceptive, Roberta picked up the food that was left on the table and carried it into the house.

Adam followed her with the salad bowl and another dish.

He put them down on the kitchen table and said:

"Why are you being so difficult?"

"I am not . . . I promise you I am not," Roberta replied. "It is just that I feel that what you are suggesting is . . . very wrong."

He raised his eye-brows and she knew he was genuinely surprised.

"How can it be wrong?" he asked. "We are both free to love each other, at least I am! I promise you I have no wife hidden away in my past, or even a permanent mistress, for that matter."

It flashed through Roberta's mind that that was what he

was asking her to be, and she could see the procession of women who had been her father's mistresses since she had been with him.

Several of them had been French, beautiful, alluring and, she thought, extremely attractive.

And yet he had tired of them so quickly that looking back it seemed to her that one moment they were there in her father's life and the next they had vanished.

Then there had been the *Contessa* from Italy, and her dark eloquent eyes were to Roberta mingled with the Churches and Temples of Rome, the candles in St. Peter's, the barges moving up the Tiber.

But the *Contessa* too had vanished on the ebb-tide with the arrival of Francine.

She, at least, had lasted for two years until she died, but Roberta with a new perception, born of what she felt for Adam, knew that while Francine had attracted, aroused and amused her father, what he felt for her had not been the love he had given her mother.

Looking back into her childhood she could remember that when her father and mother were together they had seemed to be enveloped with light.

She had always believed it was sunshine which filled the house. Now she knew it was the light of love, the light that Adam was trying to paint in his pictures.

It was the light she had felt last night when he had first kissed her and which had been part of the moonlight, part of her soul.

"That is real love!" she told herself. "The rest is only a transitory passion like the leaping flames of the fire which are extinguished, die down quickly leaving behind only dust and ashes."

Replying to his pleading she said:

"I . . . I cannot explain . . . but I cannot do what you ask."

"I do not understand. You love me!"

"How can you be...sure of...that?"

"I knew when I kissed you last night," Adam answered, "that it was not only the most wonderful kiss I had ever given and received, but that when our lips touched you became part of me, and I was no longer complete without you."

It was exactly what she felt herself, and it was almost impossible to resist him when he spoke in that deep voice that seemed to vibrate through her body.

Because she was afraid she would throw herself into his arms and tell him she would do anything he wished, she said quickly:

"I must...go to...Danny!"

Before he could stop her she had run from the kitchen across the Sitting-Room and into Danny's room.

He had undressed, got into bed, and was nearly asleep.

"I'se tired!" he said as Roberta tucked him in and knelt down beside the couch to kiss him.

"You have enjoyed yourself today," she said softly.

"It was *scrumptious!*"

"That is a new word!"

"Uncle Adam said it was *scrumptious* having you and me with him."

"It is very kind of him," Roberta said with a little throb on the words.

"I love Uncle Adam," Danny said. "I love Columbus, but most of all, I love you!"

"Thank you, darling."

She kissed him and knew as his eyes closed that he was already asleep.

She pulled the curtains across the window to shut out the last rays of the setting sun, then slowly, because she was nervous, went back into the Sitting-Room.

Adam was already there and she knew he had put the dishes in the sink for her, and what was left of the food in the larder.

He was sitting on the sofa but did not get up. He only put out his hand towards her.

"Come and sit close to me."

"Not if you are . . . going to . . . argue with . . . me."

"I will not do that. I love you too much to want you to do anything you do not wish to do, and I will wait until you are ready. But for God's sake, my precious, do not make me wait too long."

Relieved to think she had won the battle, Roberta sat down beside him, and because he obviously expected it, she put her head on his shoulder.

"I feel . . . safe here," she said in a low voice.

It was the first thought that came into her mind.

Then when his arm tightened but he did not say anything she went on:

"At the same time, if I stay, you will have to let me contribute towards Danny's and my keep. I can afford it, I promise you I can, but you know the money you obtained for your pictures will not last for ever."

"I have been thinking of that," Adam said, "and because there are so many things I want to give you I am going to finish a picture I have already started that has been ordered by an elderly woman."

The way he spoke made Roberta ask:

"Is it the sort of picture that would be recognised by the Royal Academy?"

"Exactly! Flowers! Flowers as stiff as possible in a nice china vase!"

He spoke derisively and Roberta said:

"I am sure you could paint a de Heem if you wanted to."

She thought he would take this as a compliment. Her

father had always said in his opinion the Flemish artist, Jan Davidsz de Heem painted the first flower pictures ever known.

"I have no wish to paint like de Heem," Adam said sharply. "I want to paint like Renoir, Sisley or Monet, the sort of pictures which you and I enjoy but which are apparently unsaleable."

Roberta laughed.

"And your de Heem will fetch—what?"

"Quite a number of dollars."

"Then hurry up and finish it for her," Roberta said. "Then I can feed you on beef-steaks every day, however expensive they may be!"

Adam laughed and kissed her forehead.

"You are tempting me from my appointed path!"

"It will be very rocky if you are hungry, and it would be far easier for you to accept what I have offered."

"Although I would not accept money from you, or from any other woman," Adam said seriously, "I would rather paint you than go looking for gold in the Rocky Mountains."

"It sounds exciting! Perhaps I could go with you and cook for the other gold-diggers, who the books tell me are fleeced of their nuggets by dishonest Tavern-keepers and dancing girls."

"That is true enough," Adam agreed. "The hardship the men endured would be intolerable if they had not some sort of amusement."

"Just as you would find it!"

"Of course!" he agreed.

'That is what I would be for him,' Roberta thought to herself. 'But I do not want to be an "amusement" that he can throw away when he is tired of me, just as Papa rid himself of the ladies from France and Italy, as soon as he was bored with them.'

Thinking of her father she must have stiffened, for Adam said:

"I do not want you to think of anything unpleasant. I want you to be happy, and never again do I want to see that worried expression in your eyes that you had when you first came here."

"I was very worried in case Danny and I should have to sleep under a tree for the night with only Columbus to look after us."

"I will look after you."

There was silence for a little while. Then he said:

"Did he really mean so much to you?"

"Who?"

"Your husband, of course."

Roberta hesitated.

She did not want to lie. In fact, she hated lying, especially to somebody she loved.

He was waiting for her answer and after what seemed a long pause she said:

"I . . . I do not want to . . . talk about him."

"Nor do I," Adam said. "It makes me fiercely jealous to think any man has ever touched you, or kissed you. You are mine, Roberta, mine completely! I will murder any man in the future who comes near you!"

He spoke with a violence that surprised her.

At the same time, she felt as if her whole heart leapt towards him because being near him made the world no longer a frightening place in which she and Danny were alone.

It flashed across her mind that perhaps the people from Blue River were looking for Danny, feeling it was their duty to do so, because his parents had been killed near their village.

Then she was sure she was frightening herself unnecessarily, and anyway as long as she was with Adam he would protect them, and somehow make sure that Danny was not taken from her.

His lips moved from her forehead and he kissed her eyes and the softness of her cheeks.

She wanted him to kiss her lips and she was ready, lifting her face towards his, wanting him because it was impossible not to respond to his touch.

Instead he ran his fingers along the line of her chin and gently encircled her neck with his hand.

It gave her a strange feeling which was somehow different from what she had felt before, and she could feel her heart beginning to beat in a tempestuous manner.

She knew too that his heart was beating in the same way.

Then gently, so gently she could hardly believe it was happening, he moved her down sideways onto the sofa and lifted her feet up onto it.

Then he was lying beside her and their bodies were touching.

His lips became more passionate, more demanding, and although she felt she must struggle against him, somehow it was impossible to move.

He kissed her mouth, then he was kissing the little pulse beating in her neck and again sensations which she had never dreamt existed seemed to be beating through her breast.

He held her closer and still closer, and now she could feel her heart beating against his. She knew he was growing more and more excited and she could not stop him engendering the same excitement within herself.

"I want you! God, how I want you!" Adam muttered.

Now his lips seemed to be burning with a strange fire and her body responded with flames that burnt their way through her until she felt as if they were both consumed by their violence.

Then as she felt Adam's hand on her breast she was aware of the danger she was in, not only from him, but from herself and her longing for him.

It was with superhuman effort that she pushed him away from her and somehow as he loosened his hold on her, he slipped off the sofa onto the floor.

"No! No! No!" she said, as if she was replying to something he had asked her.

He did not speak, but sat where she had pushed him, leaning on one hand and looking at her with burning eyes.

Slowly she got up from the couch. Then she said in a voice that broke:

"I . . . cannot! Oh . . . Adam . . . I . . . cannot do it!"

Although she was free she could think of nothing but her need of him and moved slowly, almost as if she was sleep-walking, across the Sitting-Room and into her own bed-room.

As she shut the door she felt as if she was shutting herself out from a Paradise she would never find again, and her whole body cried out as if it was a crime against her love.

Slowly she undressed, and only when she was in bed did she turn her face into the pillow to cry herself to sleep.

*   *   *

Roberta heard Adam moving about the Sitting-Room early the next morning.

Danny was still sleeping, but Columbus lying by the couch had his head raised and his curly tail was thumping softly on the ground.

Roberta lay still, listening to Adam's movements, longing to join him, to be beside him.

But she felt limp and defeated from the storm that had shaken her after she had gone to bed last night, her lips were dry, and she felt sure her eyes were still swollen.

"How can I be so foolish?" she asked herself. "Why do I not do as he wants?"

But she knew that while she loved him until he filled the whole earth, the sea and the sky, she could not bear to throw aside all the principles on which her mother had brought her up.

Because she had been so young they had not spoken of anything that concerned sexual immorality between men and women.

But she had known from the time she could first think that everything about her mother was good, and that the women who consoled her father after her death, even the lovely Lady Bingham, were very different in character.

Roberta was sure that her mother, however much she was attracted by another man, would never have left her husband or given up the social position in which she set an example to the people on her husband's estate and those whom he employed.

"You must always remember," her mother had said once, "that whatever we do has an influence on others."

Roberta had been quite young, but she had tried to understand.

"Just as when we are cross or disagreeable we affect those around us," her mother had gone on, "or if we do things that are wrong, this can affect someone else's life, even though we are not aware of it."

She had seen Roberta look bewildered as she explained:

"The children in the village admire you, and I am sure that if they heard that you were naughty and did things which upset your father and me, they would feel that they could behave in the same way."

Thinking about it now, Roberta thought there was nobody here in America to whom she ought to set an example or whom she could influence for right or wrong.

Then she remembered Danny.

Danny was young, but very perceptive.

How could she let him think that the aunt whom he thought his mother had sent to him from Heaven was no better than the dancing-girls who picked the pockets of the gold-miners?

'I have to be good,' she thought, and knew it would be the hardest thing she had ever done in her whole life.

When she was dressed she went into the Sitting-Room and found as she expected that Adam had set up his easel and was painting feverishly a vase of flowers which he had arranged on a small table in front of one of the windows.

She could not help smiling as she realised it was a very traditional-looking arrangement of wild flowers, but included some exotic orchids and lilies that were growing in the garden.

She had been surprised when she saw them and had asked:

"Did you plant those, Adam, or were they the choice of some previous tenant?"

"There has been no previous tenant." Adam replied. "My father gave me this house when I was at College, complaining that the noise my friends made when I was at home distracted him."

"What a lovely present!" Roberta exclaimed.

"That is what I thought when he gave it to me, because I liked bathing and boating on the sea. Then after I had been to Paris I realised it was exactly what I wanted as a Studio!"

"You did not paint before you went to France?"

"I had always enjoyed drawing and trying my hand first with water-colours and with oils. After I left College I was determined to see something of the world and I went first to London, then to Paris."

"And what did you think of Paris?"

"It was a revelation! I knew then that while I had been experimenting on my own and attempting to paint light, the Impressionists had already found a way to do so."

"And you have been painting ever since."

"I spent some time making up my mind," Adam replied, "but now I intend to do nothing else!"

There was a hard note in his voice which made Roberta suspect that it had not been an easy decision.

She did not however like to ask him too many questions, in case he should in turn question her.

She appreciated all the more the comfort of the house not only because it was his, but because it was his taste which made it so attractive and so comfortable.

Now as she walked across the soft brightly coloured rugs he did not turn to greet her as she expected, but only said in a somewhat sour voice:

"As you see, I am earning my bread and butter, and let us hope there is plenty of the latter."

She looked at the canvas and said:

"You will not believe me, but I think that is going to be a very attractive picture."

"For those who like it!"

"Exactly! I am one of them."

Adam made a derisive noise as she walked into the kitchen.

He was rather silent at breakfast and she had the feeling that he was not looking at her directly.

She knew she had offended him last night.

At the same time, there was nothing she could do about

it, and because it was the only way she could make amends she said:

"If you want a break from what you are doing, I will sit for you."

"I had better finish the damned thing and get it over," Adam replied. "I am going to San Diego tomorrow. I will leave early and be back before nightfall. Then we can spend the money on riotous living!"

"I shall enjoy that!"

He did not smile at her as she had hoped, but went back to his easel and continued to paint.

She could see that he was doing it very skillfully, and she knew that it would be quite easy, if he wished to make a lot of money, for him to paint the sort of pictures that people wanted.

She knew it was almost universal for elderly women to like flower paintings.

Her grandmother had several in her Drawing-Room, and her Aunt Emily painstakingly made tapestry covers for the Dining-Room chairs in flower designs.

Looking at Adam's handsome profile without his being aware of it, Roberta knew that his lips were set in a hard line and there was a cynical expression in his eyes.

'It is very difficult to be a revolutionary against the accepted order,' she thought, and knew that in a different way he was like her father.

But at least her father, having run away from everything that was conventional, had been rich enough to do it without any real discomfort to himself.

Adam was poor, and it was therefore more difficult for him to paint the pictures that appealed to him, while in order to live he had to, as he thought, prostitute his art.

Nevertheless when by dinner-time, the picture was finished, Roberta could admire it with complete sincerity.

"It is very attractive!" she said. "You must see that."

"I see nothing but a lot of flowers stuck stiffly into a vase, when they would look far better growing in the soil!"

Roberta laughed.

"Now you are being difficult," she said, "and please, stop punishing me because you are too proud and stuck-up to accept my humble offering of a few dollars!"

Adam looked at her, then quite suddenly he laughed.

"All right," he conceded, "you win! I will sell this picture and when we have spent all the money—but all of it—I will allow you to contribute your widow's mite to keep us all from starvation."

"That is the most sensible thing you have said for a long time," Roberta smiled, "and when you get back from San Diego, I will have a delicious and most expensive dinner waiting for you."

"To which I will contribute a bottle of champagne, if it is available. If not, the finest Californian wine you have ever tasted!"

"That is a promise, and a date!" Roberta exclaimed.

They laughed together and he put his arm around her as she walked back to the kitchen to finish cooking the supper.

Because the black mood in which he had been enveloped all day was now past, they were closer together than they had been before, and Danny joined in their laughter while surreptitiously feeding Columbus with tid-bits under the table.

Since he had been properly fed he looked a different dog from when Roberta had first seen him.

Now his coat was silky and shining, and he no longer winced away in fear if anybody approached him.

'He is happy,' Roberta thought, 'just as I am.'

Then as she saw Adam looking at her and saw the expression in his eyes, she was afraid, not of him, but of herself.

How was it going to be possible to go on resisting him, she asked, when not only her body but her heart and soul cried out for him?

She wanted him in the same way that he wanted her.

chapter six

"WHY have we got to leave, Aunt Roberta?" Danny asked plaintively for about the sixth time.

Carrying her grip in her hand and holding Danny by the other, Roberta took a minute or two to answer.

Then she said:

"I explained to you that we have to go to San Francisco, Danny."

"I don't want to go to San Francisco," Danny said crossly. "I want to stay by the sea with Uncle Adam and swim."

That was what she wished too, Roberta thought, but it was impossible to explain to the child that she knew there was nothing she could do but leave Adam.

It was frightening to think she had nowhere to go and nobody to look after her.

But she knew she was doing the right thing, and however much it hurt there could be no argument about it.

Yesterday, when she was recovering from her tears and

her unhappiness because she had upset Adam, she had only been thinking of herself.

Then last night after Danny had gone to bed she had known it was much more important that she should think about him.

She had been nervous that perhaps when he kissed her they would start the same argument all over again and she would spend another night weeping bitterly into her pillow.

When she came from the bedroom shutting the door behind her, Adam had said:

"I want to talk to you, Roberta!"

She had stood for a few moments irresolute, wondering if she would be wiser to go back into the bedroom and stay there alone.

Then as if he read her thoughts he said:

"I will not frighten you, and I will not touch you. Just sit down and listen to what I have to say."

Because he spoke in a calm, gentle voice she obeyed him and sat down on the edge of the sofa leaving a wide space between them.

She saw that he had lit the fire although it was not really necessary.

He stared into it for some minutes before he said:

"I am ashamed that I frightened you last night by being so uncontrolled."

"It . . . is all . . . right," Roberta murmured hastily.

"It is not all right," he corrected. "I behaved very badly, and I am aware of it, but my only excuse is that you made me lose my head, just as I have already lost my heart."

Now there was a note in his voice that made her quiver, but he did not look at her.

"I feel I have a lot of explaining to do," he went on, "but because you are very intelligent, I think you will understand."

"There is no reason for you to explain anything," Roberta said quickly. "I forced myself and Danny upon you, and I am sure the best thing would be for us to go away."

"How could I let that happen," Adam asked, "when you are everything I have longed for and was quite certain in my mind did not exist?"

There was a little pause. Then he added:

"When I first lived here I used to sit in front of the fire which I had lit because I felt it kept me company, and prevented me from feeling lonely."

He sounded so pathetic that Roberta wanted to put out her hands towards him, but she knew it would be a mistake and she clasped them firmly in her lap.

Then she leaned back in the corner of the sofa, as far away from him as she possibly could.

"I came here," Adam said after a moment, "to prove that I was capable of keeping myself by my painting."

He drew in his breath before he went on:

"It means everything to me, and to continue painting I would lie, cheat, steal, even risk my life rather than give it up."

He spoke in a way which would have sounded hysterical if he had raised his voice.

Instead, speaking quietly and calmly, he was expressing Roberta knew, a dedication to an ideal as he added:

"I thought if I should fail I would no longer wish to go on living."

"But you will not fail," Roberta said softly. "I am sure of it!"

"That is what I want you to say," Adam replied. "At the same time, now that you have come into my life, now that you are here, I know that you are not only a distraction, but a rival to my work."

"I . . . I am sorry," Roberta said humbly.

"You know I do not mean it like that!" Adam said sharply. "I love you until you fill my whole world! You are indivisibly part of the beauty, the light that I am trying to depict on canvas, and I could no more sever you from me than I could cut off my own arm!"

There was silence until he continued:

"At the same time, while you are an inspiration, the most beautiful person I have ever seen, part of the light that I am seeking and the centre of my existence, I am not at all certain what I can do about it."

"Why should you do . . . anything?" Roberta asked.

She did not quite understand what he was saying, and yet she knew that she wanted to help him and every word he spoke made her love him more.

Because he was not looking at her she could look at him. She knew that while he was one of the most handsome men she had ever seen, his face was different in that there was a strength and determination in it that she had never seen in any other man's face.

It gave him almost a defiant and yet at the same time a buccaneering look which was very attractive, and she thought there was also in it an expression of power.

It was the power of a man who is fighting the whole world to proclaim his own ideals, his own faith.

"I want to . . . help you."

The words seemed to come spontaneously from her lips, and even as she said them she thought he had already told her how she could help him, but that while she might inspire him, he still needed her as a woman.

There was silence after she had spoken. Then Adam said quietly:

"I cannot offer you marriage."

It was not what Roberta had expected him to say, and

she was suddenly tense. She knew that was what she wanted above everything else, and it was why she had refused to become his mistress.

"I can hardly keep myself," Adam went on, "let alone a wife and Danny, and perhaps children of my own."

"I . . . understand."

"I have to paint, you must see that! I *have* to! I quarrelled with my father and he laughed at the thought of my managing on my own without him and making a success in a different field from the one he had chosen for me."

Now there was a hardness in his voice which told Roberta without words that it had been a violent clash of temperament, and this was another reason why Adam was determined to be successful.

She did not speak and after a moment he said:

"When I am away tomorrow, I want you to think over very carefully the position we are both in. I love you, Roberta, I love you as I have never loved any woman before and I know you are an indivisible part of me that nothing and nobody can ever separate."

He gave a deep sigh.

"The position is at the moment that I can only beg you to stay with me and help me to prove myself. There is no other way that I can keep my self-respect and be faithful to my ideals."

For the first time Adam turned his face to look at her.

"I love you! I worship you!" he said. "You are everything a man could want in a woman."

His voice vibrated as he spoke and Roberta thought she could say the same thing. He was everything a woman could want in a man.

Then as they looked at each other she could see the firelight reflected in his eyes and thought they were the flames burning with him. He got up from the sofa and walked away to stand at the open window looking at the sea.

"I am not going to touch you tonight," he said. "I am not even going to kiss you. When I have gone I want you to think over what I have said, and please God, when I come back you will tell me what I want to hear."

Because he spoke so quietly the words were more moving than if he had spoken them in any other way.

Roberta clasped her hands together until the knuckles were white, forcing herself not to run to his side and throw herself into his arms.

She wanted to tell him that she loved him too, that she would stay with him, and that because they would be so happy together he would paint better than he had ever painted before.

Then as she wondered what she should say, what she should do, Adam said:

"Go to bed, my precious. It is an agony I cannot endure to keep my hands from touching you until you have thought over what I have said and made your decision."

As he spoke he opened the door onto the verandah, went out and disappeared.

For a moment Roberta could hardly believe he had really gone.

Then she knew the time for talking was over, and if she joined him he would be tempted to behave in the same way as he had last night.

Slowly she rose from the sofa, went into her bedroom, undressed and went to bed.

It was nearly two hours later that she heard Adam come back into the house, and it was then she knew that she and Danny must go away.

Whatever Adam might say they were a disrupting influence, and if they continued to live with him, since he was too proud to take money from her, he would have to paint more and more flowers for elderly women because they would pay him well for them.

"It is wrong for him, I know it is wrong!" Roberta murmured.

*　　*　　*

A few hours later when the dawn had not yet broken on the horizon she heard Adam moving about.

She listened to him, longing to get up and prepare his breakfast and kiss him goodbye, but she knew it would be a mistake.

Instead when finally she heard him leave the house she felt as if part of herself went with him, and what was left behind was a loneliness and sense of despair that was almost a physical pain.

Finding it impossible to go back to sleep she got up and started to pack her things.

After having given Danny his breakfast she told him they were going away.

At first he had not understood.

"Uncle Adam's coming back tonight, he told me so," he said. "I want to wait here for him. I want him to teach me how to swim."

"I know, darling, but we have to go away," Roberta said, "and now I want you to call me 'Aunt Roberta' again, and not 'Mama.'"

"Why?"

"Because we are going to tell the truth in future," Roberta said harshly.

She was sure it was because she had pretended to be Danny's mother that she had become embroiled so quickly in a situation from which she could extract herself only by running away.

Because of what she and Adam felt for each other she was certain that eventually the fire within them would have burst eventually into flames, even if he tried to treat her with the respect and gentleness that any decent man showed for a young girl.

Yet the wagon-driver, then Adam himself, had both thought that because she was a widow, it was easy to approach her, and it was her fault they had been deceived.

'No more lies,' she decided, 'and in San Francisco nobody will be interested as to whether Danny is my son or my cousin, which is what he is as Aunt Margaret's adopted child.'

When she was ready she had one last look around the Sitting-Room.

Perhaps she was making a mistake, she could not help wondering. Perhaps she should stay and somehow contrive that she and Danny were not a financial encumbrance on Adam.

Then she knew it would never work out that way.

It would be impossible to deceive him, and because he was fiercely proud he would never willingly accept the 'widow's mite' she had offered him.

"I have to go!" she decided.

While Danny was having his breakfast, she wrote Adam a short note which she had left on the table.

In it she said:

> *I love you with all my heart, but Danny and I must not prevent you from reaching the goal you have set yourself, and we are therefore going away.*
>
> *Perhaps later when I think you have had time to*

achieve some of the fame which will one day be yours,
I will get in touch with you.

In the meantime, I shall be praying for your suc-
cess—and missing you.

Roberta.

She put a cold supper ready for him on the kitchen table
and covered it with a linen cloth.

It was an agony to think this was the last time she could
do anything for him.

Then she told herself the sooner she took the first step
into the unknown the better.

With a protesting and reluctant Danny beside her, she
set off towards the station.

Roberta knew in which direction it lay because sometimes when they were on the beach they could hear the hoot
of the trains in the distance.

Yet it proved to be a longer walk than she had expected.

Once again she was finding her grip very heavy, and
Danny was complaining that his legs were aching before
finally she saw the station ahead of them.

It was very small and there was only one Porter in at-
tendance who stared at her curiously.

He turned out to be also the Booking-Clerk, and provided
Roberta with a ticket for herself and half-fare for Danny.

Columbus, she discovered, could travel free, but it was
strictly prohibited for him to sit on the seats.

"He is a very well-behaved dog," Roberta said with a
smile.

"In some trains the dogs have to travel in the Guard's
Van," the Porter said.

"Then I am very grateful that is not the rule on this line,"
Roberta replied.

They had to wait for half-an-hour before the train arrived which was fortunately going all the way to San Francisco.

There were already quite a number of people aboard, and Roberta learnt the train had come from San Diego and stopped at all the smaller stations on the way.

She thought it would be too extravagant to travel First Class, and therefore the carriage in which they found themselves had other passengers in it.

It certainly was not so well unholstered or as comfortable as the carriage in which Roberta had travelled from New Orleans.

The other passengers seemed friendly and the men said: "Howdy, Ma'am!" and lifted the brim of their hats to her.

Roberta sat Danny next to the window so that he could see out and she took a seat that was between him and a man who was poring over a book.

Roberta wished she too had brought something with her to read which might prevent her from remembering that the train was carrying her further and further away from Adam and she would never see him again.

The idea made her want to cry and she forced herself to talk to Danny about the beautiful countryside through which they were passing and thus try to distract her attention from her thoughts.

Danny was interested in the view only for a little while.

Then he called Columbus up beside him and putting his arms round his neck, whispered to him in a way that Roberta remembered he had done when he was hiding in the wood.

It made her remember what a lot of things had happened since her father had died, and how frightening it was to be going to a strange city having no idea where she would stay or whom she could ask for advice.

Without really meaning to she looked at the book over which the man next to her was poring and realised to her surprise that he was translating Arabic into English.

She saw there were technical terms, concerned, she thought, with trains, and almost without meaning to, she read what he had written in English from the Arabic words.

It did not make sense and impulsively without thinking that she might be intruding, she said:

"Excuse me, but that word you have just translated is wrong."

The man turned his head to stare at her and she saw he was quite young, about thirty, wearing spectacles and looked, she thought, like a Clerk.

"Wrong?" he said. "Are you saying that you can read Arabic?"

"Quite well," Roberta replied, "and the word you have just written down as 'letter' means actually: 'correspondent.'"

He stared at her as if he could not believe what he was hearing and she explained:

"'Mukatib' is 'correspondent' and 'maktub' is 'letter'!"

The young man looked down at what he had written and said:

"Thank you! Thank you very much for being so helpful!"

"It is not surprising that everyone becomes confused when they first try to speak Arabic," Roberta said, "because there are two sorts: The Classical Arabic and the Arabic of the Koran which is used frequently today, especially in commercial circles."

The man looked down at the paper on which he had been writing and said:

"I should be very grateful, Ma'am, if you would see if I have translated any other words incorrectly."

"I am afraid there are quite a lot," Roberta said after a quick look.

The man pushed the piece of paper towards her and

without speaking handed her his pencil.

Roberta realised that he was trying to translate a letter, and it was from somebody in Africa asking about a Locomotive he wished to buy.

The letter was as usual flowery and the sense of it somewhat difficult to follow, but when she had finished she understood that the correspondent was writing on behalf of one Sheik Mahmud el Akbar who was interested in acquiring a railway train and in particular a very fast and up-to-date engine.

She could see the young man who had been told to translate the letter had made a somewhat misleading mess of it.

Roberta could speak Arabic more fluently than she could write, and she wished Francine was with her who would have found not only the literal translation easy, but would have subtly altered it into more understandable form.

Nevertheless, by the time she had finished which took her a little time, the translation was both intelligible and accurate, and as she handed it to the young man he was so profuse in his thanks that she felt he was almost ready to cry in gratitude.

"It is difficult to thank you enough, Ma'am," he said over and over again. "If I had failed to do properly what I had been told, I might easily have found myself out of a job!"

Roberta smiled.

"I cannot believe your employer could be as unfeeling as that!"

He gave a sharp laugh that had no humour in it.

"You must have heard of Mr. Theodore Garson?"

"Is that your employer?" Roberta enquired. "I am afraid the name means nothing to me."

The young man stared at her in astonishment.

"Nothing to you?" he repeated. "But everybody knows Mr. Theodore Garson!"

"Why?" Roberta asked. "Is he the Governor of California or the Mayor of San Francisco?"

The young man laughed again.

"No, indeed much more important than that! Mr. Theodore Garson owns this Railroad, and he is the biggest Railroad owner in the whole State!"

"Oh, now I understand!" Roberta exclaimed.

She had learnt from the books she had read that those who ran the Railways thought of themselves as gods and behaved as such.

"So it is Mr. Garson who is selling a railway train to an Arab!" she said.

As she spoke she thought it was typical that one of the rich and important Sheiks should want to buy a railway train.

He had doubtless heard a great deal about them, and she was sure if he did acquire a train it would be a long time before he had the rails to run it on, or the facilities of a station.

Nevertheless it would be a prize possession and one that would bring him much prestige and admiration amongst his followers.

Because she was curious she could not help asking:

"Why did Mr. Garson not find an Arab to translate the Sheik's letter for him?"

"He expected it to be done in his own office," the young man replied, "and he wanted it translated within twenty-four hours!"

"Without your knowing Arabic?" Roberta exclaimed. "It was an impossible task!"

"That's what we thought, but when Mr. Garson says something has to be done, it's done."

Roberta looked at the book he had handed her and saw that it was a very old, rather out-of-date Arab Dictionary.

"This was the only book I could find in Arabic," the young man said apologetically.

"I am not surprised that you found the translation difficult," she said. "So many Arabic words look alike and sometimes have two or three different meanings according to the context in which they are spoken."

The young man gave a sigh. Then he said:

"Perhaps, Ma'am, if it's not too much to ask, if there's another letter waiting for me in the office when I get there, I could give it to you."

"Of course, I should be very pleased to help you," Roberta replied, "but as yet I do not know where I shall be staying in San Francisco."

"You're new to the City?"

"I have never been there before. In fact, I am English."

"English!" the young man exclaimed. "I thought you had a funny accent, but I couldn't place it."

Roberta was tempted to retort that it was he who had the funny accent, but then she thought it might seem rude.

As if he must make certain of her help, he told her how frightening it was to work in an office that belonged to the great Theodore Garson.

The young man's name was Bert Weingart and he had only been employed for the last three months by Mr. Garson and was terrified of being sacked for incompetence.

"I know very little about Railroads," he said, "but I'm proficient in French, which is important in our dealings with New Orleans, and I can also speak Italian and Mexican, and am contriving to learn Chinese."

Roberta laughed.

"Now I can understand why Mr. Garson would expect

you to find no difficulty in reading Arabic, and I am sure Chinese is much more difficult."

"I'm really only a beginner," Bert said modestly.

"I think it is very enterprising of you to study it at all," Roberta replied, "and while I can speak Arabic, I have no wish to learn Chinese."

At the same time, she knew there were a great number of Chinese living in San Francisco.

Her books had told her they kept very much to themselves, and she did not expect to come in contact with them.

When she talked to Bert Weingart he told her how many different nationalities were represented among the inhabitants.

"Most of them came with the Gold Rush," he explained, "people from every country all over the world, and they are now assimilated into local life."

The Germans and the Hungarians had planted vineyards, many Italians had become fishermen and still used their felucca boats for crab-fishing in San Francisco Bay.

By the time Bert had talked of other Italians who had founded the first packing corporation and opened Restaurants and the Chocolate Factory, the Irish who had become Policemen, Firemen and Catholic Clergy, and the French who had a separate Colony of their own like the Chinese, Roberta felt as if her head was spinning.

Now she was even more frightened of going to San Francisco than she had been when she started.

'If everything is too terrifying,' she thought consolingly, 'we can always go back to Adam.'

Then she told herself severely that that was something she should never do.

At the same time, by the time the train had reached the outskirts of the City and she could see the Pacific Ocean on one side of the railway line, and San Francisco Bay on the other, she had a wild impulse to turn round and go back to the safety of Adam's arms.

Then she remembered his arms were far from safe where she was concerned, and told herself she had to be brave and face what years later would seem an adventure.

It was then that Bert Weingart, still overcome with gratitude said:

"If it's not an impertinent question to ask, Ma'am, where are you and the little boy going to stay tonight?"

"I was just going to ask you to recommend a quiet Hotel," Roberta replied.

He thought for a moment. Then he said:

"I know my mother would be very pleased to put you up. Our house is not large, but she'll make you comfortable."

"That is very kind of you," Roberta said. "But . . ."

She was just about to say that perhaps she and Danny would be better on their own when she asked herself why not?

At least it would give her time to find out from Mrs. Weingart how they could either find lodgings, or perhaps, when she could obtain some money from England, an apartment.

She knew that Danny had to go to School and she was determined to find something for herself to do during the long hours when he would not be with her.

There had been nothing definite in her mind, however, and now, because she knew quite a number of languages she thought she might easily be useful as an Interpreter, at least as far as Arabic was concerned.

As if Bert was thinking along the same lines he said:

"I'm really being selfish because I'm so afraid you'll disappear and there might be half-a-dozen letters from the

Sheik waiting for me when I get to the office. Without you, what should I do?"

Roberta thought this was actually a very sensible question, but she merely said:

"I should be very grateful if it would not be a nuisance for your mother to have us to stay for the night and tomorrow I can look around for somewhere else."

"I'm sure my mother'll be able to help you," Bert answered.

It was certainly a great help to have him when they arrived at the station.

He procured a carriage for them and they set off to drive first down a very steep hill, then up another in a way that Roberta found quite bewildering.

She had been told that San Francisco was built on seven hills, but she had not realised how fantastic it would be, or how strange to go up and down as if one way, she thought, on an enormous switch-back.

What she did quickly realise was that San Francisco was beautiful, and even Danny exclaimed with excitement as the horse drew them down a long steep hill with trees on each side of it, then up another one even steeper.

Some of the homes were designed in a very elaborate style and these Roberta learnt later, were known as "fancy-work" homes.

They were all angles and florid garniture, eccentric and scrappy as a crazy quilt. She wanted to laugh at them but thought Bert might be offended.

They finally stopped in an unimportant-looking road where the houses were, Roberta guessed, comparatively cheap.

When she was ushered in by Bert she saw the Living-Room was spotlessly clean and was sure the moment she saw Mrs. Weingart that she was of German origin.

She was certainly very friendly, and when Bert explained

how kind and helpful Roberta had been she thanked her as eloquently as he had done.

Food appeared as if my magic—hot biscuits, Apfel Strüdel, a heavy Plum Cake, strawberry tart and there was milk for Danny to drink and coffee for Roberta.

She was obviously expected to tell Mrs. Weingart about herself and she told the truth.

She did not say she had a title, but she explained that her father had died in Algiers and she had therefore come out to America to stay with his favourite sister who had married an American Preacher.

She told her about Clint Dulaine and finished by saying that she was looking after Danny until he had finished a tour of the State.

She did not tell Mrs. Weingart that he had gone back to itinerant preaching, but merely implied that he was on some sort of mission on behalf of the Episcopal Church.

They did not think it strange that she and Danny were travelling alone, and Mrs. Weingart merely suggested that Bert should enquire at the office if Roberta could be asked formally to interpret any correspondence which came from Africa.

"It would be no use, son, your pretending you can do it when you can't," she said. "'Tell the truth and shame the Devil,' is what I always say, and no harm can come to you from that!"

"I don't think Mr. Garson would employ a woman, Mama," Bert said uneasily.

"She wouldn't need to sit in the office," Mrs. Weingart retorted. "You could bring the letters to her for translation then take them back again. What would it matter to him, so long as he has his letters done right?"

Roberta knew Bert was thinking of how incorrect his

efforts at translation had been and he said a little reluctantly:

"All right. I'll do what you suggest, Mama, but if he bawls me out, it'll be your fault!"

"I can bear it," Mrs. Weingart said dryly. "But I do not suppose it will be easy to find anybody else who speaks as many languages as you do."

Bert smiled at this and Roberta realised he was very proud of his accomplishments.

"I think it is wonderful of your son to try to learn Chinese," she said. "I have always been told it is one of the most difficult languages in the world."

"Bert is a tryer like his father," Mrs. Weingart said proudly, "and he's not easily defeated."

She then took Roberta and Danny up the stairs and showed them two tiny rooms where they could sleep which were sparsely furnished, but like the rest of the house spotlessly clean.

An hour later there was a large meal to which Danny did full justice, although Roberta found it impossible to eat very much of the rich meat stew with huge dumplings and the peach pie which followed it.

Bert's father was a large bald man who spoke with a heavy German accent, even though it was many years since he had lived in his native land.

He now ran a small Sausage Factory which brought in, Roberta learnt, quite a comfortable income on which to live so that they did not need to expand it any further.

"Bert could never bear the smell of the factory, even when he was a little boy," Mrs. Weingart explained when her husband was not listening. "Then as he did so well at School it seemed a waste to put him somewhere where his gift for languages would not be appreciated."

"Yes, of course," Roberta murmured.

"We were lucky to get him into Mr. Garson's office. He is a hard man—there is no gainsaying that—but it's a privilege to work for him."

Roberta heard so much about Mr. Garson that she began to think he loomed over Bert's life like some frightening Ogre.

She was therefore somewhat apprehensive when the following afternoon he came back from work to say that Mr. Garson wished to see her.

"To see me?" Roberta exclaimed.

"When I told him how you helped me to translate the letter," Bert said, "at first he bawled me out because I hadn't been able to do it myself. Then when I explained how difficult a language Arabic was and he read what you had corrected he said he wanted to see you."

"Did you not say that I would be happy for you to bring me the work to translate so that I could do them while I was here?" Roberta asked.

"I told him that," Bert said, "but he just said he would send a carriage for you. You are to go to his house which is outside the City, and be ready by four o'clock."

Because it was nearly that time already Roberta ran upstairs to put on her bonnet and Danny followed her.

"You stay here, darling, until I come back," she said to him.

"I want to come with you, Aunt Roberta."

She did not answer and after a moment Danny went on pleadingly:

"Please let me come with you. Columbus and I can stay in the carriage and wait, but I don't want to be left here alone."

She knew perceptively that it was not because he did not like the Weingarts, but because he was afraid he might lose her.

Like all children who have been upset by constant chopping and changing in their lives, he was now clinging to the one person who seemed stable, and that was herself.

She smiled at him.

"Of course you can come," she said, "but I am afraid you will have to sit in the carriage and not run about the garden, if there is one."

"I'll be very good!" Danny promised.

At the appointed time they were travelling once again up and down the fascinating roads.

Roberta had arranged with Mrs. Weingart that she would stay with her for a few days while she looked around for a furnished apartment she might rent, and she was told there were quite a number of them available.

Accordingly, first thing in the morning she had gone to the Bank recommended by Bert's father, and having demanded to see the Manager, explained to him who she was.

She produced a copy of her father's Will, the letters to his Bank in London and one she had already written asking that quite a considerable amount of money should be transferred to San Francisco and deposited in her name.

The Bank Manager was very helpful, but at the same time Roberta knew he was extremely curious about her.

Because it seemed a wise thing to do she explained that she had come out to live with her aunt Lady Margaret Dulaine, only to find that she had died.

"I feel I have heard the name Dulaine quite recently," the Bank Manager said. "Now what was it I read?"

He concentrated for a moment, then rang a bell on his desk and said to the Clerk who answered it:

"Bring me yesterday's newspaper."

"Which one, Sir?"

"The *Herald*."

The Clerk disappeared and the Bank Manager said:

"We have a large number of newspapers published in the City in many different languages, and it is always hard to remember which one I was reading. But I feel certain in this case it was the 'Herald.'"

A minute later the Clerk brought it in, and he turned over the pages, then gave an exclamation and said:

"I am sorry, Lady Roberta, but I am afraid I have bad news for you."

He passed her the newspaper and she read:

DEATH IN THE ROCKY MOUNTAINS

Bill Evans, a Prospector working on his own, was found by a Preacher, Mr. Clint Dulaine, incapacitated with a broken leg after a fall in a storm. Mr. Dulaine attempted to carry the man to safety, but they were both swept by the wind into a gully, and crashed down into a swollen river.

It was thought that Mr. Dulaine with great courage attempted to save his companion's life, but both men were swept away over a cascade and drowned.

Roberta read the paragraph twice before she said:

"As you will understand this is a shock, although I never met Mr. Dulaine...I was hoping to meet him when he returned to his home in Blue River."

"I am deeply sorry to be the bearer of bad news, Lady Roberta," the Manager said.

Roberta thought for a moment. Then she said:

"As both my aunt and Mr. Dulaine are now dead, I should be very grateful if you would not mention to anybody from Blue River where I am, should they by any chance get in touch with you."

"I understand your feelings in not wishing to be involved

now that there is no necessity for it," the Bank Manager said, "and I can promise you that I will carry out your wishes."

"Thank you."

Roberta signed the papers he produced, told him she would be at Mr. and Mrs. Weingart's house until she could find somewhere else to live, then left.

He told her she could immediately draw any money she needed from the Bank, but she assured him she had enough for the time being, which was true.

She had, before she left Adam's house, taken some of the larger notes out of the hem of her skirt where she had hidden them, but she had also left several behind in case she might have her pocket picked or lose the bag in which she habitually carried her money.

As she left the Bank she thought that if she had not been sure before, she knew now that Danny belonged to her and he was her responsibility.

Whatever she did, wherever she went, she would look after the little boy, and nobody should take him from her.

She found herself wishing however that she could tell Adam what had happened, and she knew because he had been so kind to Danny he would know how to comfort him.

"I *have* to manage on my own!" she told herself bravely.

She knew it would not be the same as having Adam to rely on and Adam to advise her what was best for the boy.

It was touching the way Danny clung to her, and when they had driven for several miles outside the City she knew as they turned in through the drive gates of what appeared to be a large house he was still nervous that he might lose her.

"You won't forget about me, Aunt Roberta, will you?" he asked.

"No, of course not!" she smiled. "The carriage has to

take me home and I would certainly not want to walk all that way back to the City!"

Danny laughed.

"Your legs would get very tired."

"Very, very tired," Roberta agreed. "So I promise you, after I have seen the gentleman who wishes to speak to me, we will go back together."

She thought he looked wistfully through the carriage window at the garden through which they were passing, but she knew he would stay where he was as she had told him to do.

The house was two-storeyed, extensive and attractive, built of white stone and in a style reminiscent of California's Spanish-Mexican era.

A servant opened the door and when Roberta said she was expected he smiled.

"You look too young to be working for the Master!" he said.

The way he spoke made Roberta realise he was not being familiar, as such a remark would have been coming from an English servant, but merely friendly.

"I am older than I look!" she replied, and he laughed.

"I can believe my eyes, can't I?" he enquired, which made Roberta laugh too.

They walked along some wide and lofty passages, until as the servant drew nearer to the door at the end of them he was silent, and Roberta had the feeling he was just as much in awe of Mr. Garson as Bert was.

He opened the door and announced:

"The young woman you were expecting, Mr. Garson!"

Sitting at a large desk piled with papers was a man whom Roberta knew at once was exactly the type to inspire awe and fear in those who worked for him.

He was going grey at the temples, but his eye-brows

which almost met across his nose were dark. His chin was very square, and his lips set in a tight line.

As she approached the desk Mr. Garson looked at her with eyes that she felt were both penetrating and suspicious, almost as if he felt she intended to impose on him.

Then as he did not speak she said:

"Good-evening! You asked me to come to see you."

"I *sent* for you," he corrected sharply, "because the young fool in my office who is supposed to be a linguist tells me you speak Arabic."

"He told you correctly," Robert replied. "I have been living in North Africa until recently and I can therefore speak Arabic quite fluently."

Mr. Garson made a sound that she thought was slightly derogatory, before he asked:

"How can I be sure of that?"

Roberta looked at him in surprise.

"You can test me by asking me to translate something else for you, as I have already done," she replied, "or find somebody who also speaks Arabic to judge my efficiency."

She could not help thinking as she spoke that he might find this difficult, since Bert had told her that as far as he knew, there were no Arabs living in San Francisco.

Mr. Garson did not answer and after a moment Roberta looked at the chair in front of the desk in a meaningful way.

"You had better sit down," he said as if she had prompted him.

"Thank you, that is very kind of you," Roberta replied. "And now, Mr. Garson, perhaps you will tell me exactly why you have asked me to come here."

The question seemed to take him by surprise and after a moment he replied:

"I understand you wanted to translate my letters for me!"

"I will certainly consider such an offer of employment,"

Roberta said quietly, "but as I have only just arrived in San Francisco, I might find something more attractive for me to do."

She knew with amusement that Mr. Garson was taken aback by her reply.

She was sure he believed that because he was so rich everybody was anxious to work for him and would crawl pleadingly at his feet if he asked them to do so.

"Where are you staying?" he enquired abruptly.

"At Mr. and Mrs. Weingart's house. Bert's father and mother were kind enough to put me up last night," Roberta answered, "but I am looking for an apartment of my own and intend to start searching for one tomorrow."

There was silence. Then Mr. Garson said:

"I cannot hang about waiting for letters to be translated into Arabic while you look around for an apartment. So for the moment you had better come here!"

Now he certainly surprised Roberta and she looked at him in astonishment.

"Here?" she questioned.

"There is plenty of room, and I need you on hand when I want you," he said "I am not having you interfering in the office, turning all the young men's heads, and making them waste their time when they should be working."

"I have no intention of working in your office, Mr. Garson," Roberta said quietly, "and I think perhaps it would be a mistake for me to stay here, although it was very kind of you to invite me."

She could not help feeling as she spoke that it would be lovely for Danny to be out in the country instead of in the town.

"I want you here!" Mr. Garson answered sharply. "I have no time to go all over the City with every letter which arrives here."

"No, I quite understand that," Roberta agreed.

"I will not see you unless I want to," he remarked almost as if he was reasoning it out for himself. "You can come at once. I will send the carriage for your things."

He gave her a glance over the top of the paper he was holding and Roberta thought with amusement that he was quite expecting her to settle down and work all night.

"It certainly sounds a very interesting idea," she said slowly, "but I will have to bring somebody with me."

"Somebody? Who do you mean, a man? I thought you were unmarried."

"I am," Roberta replied, "but I have a little boy with me, a relation whom I am looking after."

"Boys? I will not have boys about the place making a noise and a mess!"

Roberta smiled.

"That is what I thought you would say."

She rose to her feet.

"I will of course help you out if you are unable to find anybody else to translate your letters," she said, "and when I leave Mrs. Weingart, I will let Bert know where I am staying."

As she finished speaking she walked towards the door and only when she had reached it did Mr. Garson shout:

"Where do you think you are going?"

"I thought we had finished our discussion."

For a moment it seemed as if he could not force the words to his lips. Then Mr. Garson growled:

"Where is this boy? In the City?"

"No, he is outside waiting in the carriage you sent for me."

Again there was silence before almost like the roar of a lion Mr. Garson shouted:

"Bring him in. Let me have a look at him."

Roberta smiled and opened the door and walked back down the passage.

The servant was waiting in the hall and as he opened the front door for her she said:

"Mr. Garson wants to see the little boy I have with me."

She thought the servant's expression of astonishment was almost farcical.

Then as she saw Danny looking out through the window of the carriage she called:

"Come here, Danny!"

He opened the carriage door and jumped out with Columbus at his heels.

"The gentleman who owns this house wants to meet you," she said.

She took Danny by the hand and they walked along the high corridors and the servant, who had followed them, opened the door into Mr. Garson's Study.

He seemed to be busy at his desk, but Roberta had the feeling that he was waiting for them with curiosity.

She could see his eyes under their dark eye-brows staring at Danny as they walked towards him.

Then to her astonishment Danny ran round the desk, not in the least nervous, and said to Mr. Garson:

"Bert says you are building the fastest train-engine in the whole world! Please, will you show it to me?"

Roberta had no idea that Danny had listened to the conversation in which Bert had explained about the special Locomotive which Mr. Garson was planning to build, and which was to be larger and faster than any other engine in the whole of America.

"It will be sensational!" Bert had said. "An Express to beat every other Express, and his rivals will be biting their nails with fury when they know about it!"

"What do you know about my engine?" Mr. Garson asked gruffly.

"That it's going to be faster than any other engine, and I want to ride in it," Danny said, "and when I'm big, I'll drive it for you."

"Why are you interested in trains?" Mr. Garson enquired.

"Because they're so exciting, and I want to go fast, very, very fast, but safely so that people aren't killed, but at the same time they can go wherever they want in America and very quickly!"

"That is the most sensible explanation I have heard for some time," Mr. Garson said. "What is your name, young man?"

"Everybody calls me 'Danny,' but I was christened 'Daniel.'"

It struck Roberta that an earlier Daniel had bearded a great lion in his den and incredible though it seemed that was what Danny was doing to Mr. Garson.

To her astonishment he brought a large plan out of one of the drawers of his desk and spread it out for Danny to see.

The small boy asked intelligent questions and Mr. Garson was ready to answer them seriously.

When he was explaining that it would be faster than any other engine, Danny gave a deep sigh.

"It's a *gorgeous* train!" he said. "Absolutely *gorgeous!* Please, may I travel in it when you have built it? Please, please!"

It would have been difficult for anybody even with a heart of stone, Roberta thought, to refuse Danny's wide pleading eyes and eager face.

He was such an attractive little boy and she could understand that just as she had been, Mr. Garson for all his gruff exterior was captivated by him.

"Perhaps you may be the first to travel on my engine," he said as he showed him the plans, "but I will tell you one thing, young man, you are the first person who is not in the business to see these plans, and I have enemies who would like to be in your place because they would steal them from me, if they could!"

"Do you mean they would then build the engine and not you?" Danny asked.

"Exactly!" Mr. Garson said, "so you must keep what you have seen very secret. Do you understand?"

"I promise you I will explain it to nobody!" Danny said.

He went a little nearer to Mr. Garson.

"You did say I would be the first person to ride in it?"

"That is what I said," Mr. Garson said, "but of course by the time it is finished you may not be here!"

Roberta looked across the desk at Mr. Garson.

"All right," he said. "Have it your own way. The place is big enough. I do not suppose I shall hear the noise he makes!"

Almost as if he noticed Columbus for the first time and wanted to assert his authority he said:

"But no dogs! I will not have any dogs in this house!"

Danny gave a little cry and put his hand on Mr. Garson's arm.

"Columbus is not an ordinary dog," he said. "He is a very good, very quiet dog, and if you do not like him he will hide so that you will not see him."

"He can go into a kennel," Mr. Garson said firmly.

"Then I shall have to live in a kennel too," Danny said "and then you might forget about me and send the train off the first time it runs without me."

He looked up at Mr. Garson and as if he knew he was

having to battle not only on behalf of himself but also for Columbus, he said:

"Please, Columbus will be no trouble to you, and I have to look after him, as he looks after me."

"We will give it a try," Mr. Garson said sharply, "but if there is any noise, or you upset me, then you all leave. Is that understood?"

"Perhaps it is a risk we should not take," Roberta said provocatively.

"Good God, Woman! You have got what you want!" Mr. Garson snapped. "A boy and a dog! What more can I agree to?"

Roberta laughed.

"I promise you there will be no trouble, and I really do speak Arabic well enough to make sure that the Arab who is buying the train will not 'pull a fast one' on you."

She thought there was a little twitch at the corner of Mr. Garson's mouth at the way she spoke. Then he said:

"All right. Send the carriage back for your clothes and find my Housekeeper. Tell her to show you to your rooms, but mind I do not hear that dog barking."

"He will not bark unless somebody comes to try to steal the plans of the train," Danny said. "Then I will tell him to bark very, very loud, and bite the burglars too!"

Before Mr. Garson could speak Roberta said:

"You see, Mr. Garson, you are not only gaining an Interpreter but also a Security Guard and a Police dog at the same time!"

She thought he was going to laugh. Then it was as if he forced himself to say gruffly:

"I think I must be off my head!"

"On the contrary, I am sure it is something you will never regret," Roberta said, "and when we have found our rooms I will come back here so that you can give me the letters you want translated."

"All right! But do not be long about it!"

He spoke as if he had suddenly remembered that he should assert his authority and added:

"I want quite a lot done before tomorrow morning!"

"I will do what I can," Roberta promised. "Come along, Danny."

She thought he was going to follow her. Instead he slipped his hand into Mr. Garson's.

"I am glad we are coming here to you," he said. "I think you are very, very clever to design such a big engine. It's going to be very fast, the fastest in the world! And when I ride in it with you, everybody will cheer and wave."

"I hope you are right," Mr. Garson said. "There is always the chance that it may not work as well as it should."

"I will help you," Danny said confidently.

"Thank you," Mr. Garson said simply.

Then Danny was running towards Roberta with Columbus beside him.

"We're going to go so fast, Aunt Roberta," he said excitedly, "that everybody will think we have magic wings. Just think of it! The fastest train in the world—and I will be on it!"

chapter seven

"YOU can go into the garden, Danny," Roberta said, "but do not go near the part of the house where Mr. Garson works. You know he does not like noise."

"Columbus and I never make a sound when Mr. Garson is at home," Danny replied.

This was true, but Roberta had been astonished by the way in which Danny had attached himself to the awe-inspiring Tycoon.

She was aware, perhaps because of the way the Minister had treated him, that he was nervous of Mr. Weingart and also of Bert.

But Mr. Garson was different.

Although Danny was very good and kept out of sight if Mr. Garson was working, he waited for him in the hall when he came back in the evenings and would run to him eagerly asking questions about the engine and how far it had developed since the day before.

159

To Roberta's astonishment and that of everybody else in the house, Mr. Garson did not seem to mind.

He would talk to Danny about the engine, answer his questions, and reiterate his promise that he should be one of the first persons to ride in it when it was finished.

He was certainly very kind to the child but after a week of working for the man who she had learnt was the most exacting in the whole of San Francisco, Roberta knew that he certainly intended to have his money's-worth.

"I will pay you what I pay young Weingart," he said gruffly the first morning after she had arrived, "and as you get your bed and board for nothing you are doing well out of the deal!"

"I only hope I shall give satisfaction," Roberta said with mock humility.

But the irony with which she spoke was lost on Mr. Garson and he merely replied:

"If you do not, you will go!"

She found however that there was such an enormous back-log of letters from Africa that it would take her some time to sort them out and also translate those which arrived nearly every day.

It was difficult for Mr. Garson to understand that a great deal of the correspondence consisted merely of flowery expressions of politeness which had little to do with the main objective, which was to buy a train.

It had taken the Arabs some time to realise that the train involved a great many other pieces of equipment.

Roberta found it difficult not only to make clear to Mr. Garson what was wanted, but also to reply so that the Arabs would understand what was imperative for them to purchase.

Actually she found it very interesting, but she thought now as she looked at Danny running into the sunshine that she would like to be with him.

Or rather, if she was truthful, with Danny and Adam, running down the beach to swim in the sea.

She thought about Adam constantly, so that she not only found it hard to sleep at night, but would often cry despairingly feeling that she would never see him again.

She might think he painted well, and undoubtedly there would be a certain number of people, even if they had no money to buy pictures, who would appreciate his talent in France.

Yet she was quite certain that in San Francisco the Impressionist style would leave those who wanted pictures unmoved.

They would much prefer a painting of flowers or, because they were so near the sea, of the ships with their tall white sails which filled the harbour.

"Oh, Adam, Adam!" she had sobbed last night. "I want you, and Danny wants you too!"

She had not yet looked for a School for Danny, feeling that since he had been unsettled it would be a mistake for him to have to enter yet another new world in which he would be a stranger.

He seldom spoke about the School at Blue River, but she knew it had been very much a part of his life.

Now she was sure, because he was still rather small for his age and still suffering from the semi-starvation inflicted by the Minister, that it would be best for him to acclimatise himself in San Francisco before she made any more changes.

She had no idea how long Mr. Garson would keep her, and she had no wish for Danny to start at one School out here in the country, then have to move into the City and begin all over again at another.

'I wish I had somebody to advise me what is best for him,' she worried, and knew that somebody was Adam.

He would understand, he would help her, and she thought

that what Danny was looking for was a father-figure which for the moment he had found in Mr. Garson and his fast train.

She had not told him very much about Clint Dulaine, but when she made much of the courageous way he had died, Danny was not as upset as she feared.

However, she was sure it added to his feeling of insecurity and afterwards he clung to her even more closely than he had before.

She had received a letter from the Bank Manager telling her that he had sent instructions on her behalf to London and as soon as he received a reply he would contact her again.

He had addressed the letter to the Weingart house, and Bert had sent it to her by the office messenger who brought Mr. Garson's mail to the house.

She was rather perturbed when she realised the Bank Manager had naturally addressed her by her title since she had not instructed him to do otherwise.

"It will mean nothing to them!" Roberta told herself and decided that as long as she was in San Francisco it would be best just to be known as 'Miss Worth'.

Now as she walked along the passage to Mr. Garson's Study she was thinking only of Danny and feeling happy that he was looking so much healthier.

Although he had nobody to play with except Columbus, he seemed quite content, and he was certainly enjoying the very good food which the Housekeeper provided for them.

They did not eat with Mr. Garson, but in a small room off the Dining-Room where they were alone.

It was what Roberta preferred, just as she was thankful she had an office to herself next to Mr. Garson's Study, and did not have to share it with anybody else.

She was just about to go into it now when one of Mr.

162

Garson's personal Secretaries who did not live in the house came from the Study to say:

"The Master wants you, Miss Worth!"

He spoke in a somewhat ominous way and Roberta wondered what was wrong.

She went into the Study and saw Mr. Garson sitting at his desk looking down at a piece of paper he held in his hand.

He looked up at her from under his bushy eye-brows and said:

"I have been just speaking to the servants about the security of this house. I understand that one of the doors into the garden was left open last night. Was that you or the boy?"

"It was neither of us," Roberta replied. "Danny did not go outside after supper, but one of the servants was kind enough to take Columbus out last night because I was tired and wanted to go to bed early."

Mr. Garson's lips tightened.

"Lies, lies! That is all I ever get from my staff," he shouted furiously. "Nobody tells the truth, nobody owns up if they do anything wrong! Why the hell can I not be better served?"

"If you want me to be frank," Roberta answered, "I think it is because they are so frightened of you."

He looked at her in surprise before he said:

"That is no excuse for lying!"

"Of course it is," Roberta retorted. "If people are really frightened, they will say anything to get themselves out of trouble. You must be aware that you terrify everybody who works for you."

"Except you!"

"I am frightened sometimes," Roberta admitted, "but at least I am not afraid of being turned out into the street because I can afford to keep myself."

She spoke without thinking and Mr. Garson raised his eye-brows.

"You have money of your own?"

"Enough not to be so frightened that I would not tell the truth!" Roberta answered.

Unexpectedly he laughed.

"You amuse me, Miss Worth," he said. "At the same time you must be aware that my rivals would give a very great deal of money to get their hands on the plans of my new engine."

"You must make sure they do not do that."

"I have beaten them before, and I will do so again!" Mr. Garson said. "But there is no use bolting the door after the horse has been stolen! This house must be better guarded and that is an order!"

"I promise you that Danny and I will both be very careful when we take Columbus out at night to shut the door and lock it when we come in."

"That is what I expect," Mr. Garson said briefly.

As if the subject was exhausted and he had no more to say about it he handed her a letter which had arrived that morning from the Sheik.

"What is he asking for now?" he enquired abruptly.

*　　*　　*

It was late in the afternoon when Roberta, who was just finishing writing a long letter to the Sheik, realised she could hear Danny's voice in the next room.

He had been told very firmly not to disturb Mr. Garson or try to see him unless he was sent for, and for the moment she felt she must be mistaken.

Then apprehensively, in case the child was being a nuisance, she rose to her feet and went into the Study.

To her surprise Danny was sitting on Mr. Garson's knee and they were both poring over the plans for the engine that were spread out on the desk.

They were so absorbed in what they were doing that they did not notice she was there, and after a moment she withdrew silently leaving the door ajar.

She could hear Danny asking what seemed to her to be extremely intelligent questions, and Mr. Garson answering them patiently and slowly.

'I suppose what he really needs is a family of his own,' she thought. 'What a pity he has no son to inherit his vast Empire, and at the same time work with him on new projects like the fast engine.'

Danny talked about it so much that she sometimes felt she could build the engine herself and certainly could draw it with a great deal of accuracy.

Mechanics, she told herself, fascinated all men, except of course Adam, and yet in his own way he was just as dedicated as Mr. Garson was.

She gave a deep sigh, thinking that women were very much at a disadvantage when it came to a man thinking of his career and being determined to succeed.

When she thought about Adam it seemed a century since she had seen him, and her whole being yearned for him so deeply that she felt it was impossible to stay away from him.

One day she was sure, she would be able to bear it no longer and would have to go back, even if just to ask him if he still loved her.

"I love him! I love him!" she thought despairingly.

Now the tears in her eyes blurred her vision so that she could no longer see the letter she had written in Arabic.

Later that night when she should have been asleep because she was so tired, she lay in the darkness thinking of Adam, feeling as if his arms were around her, his lips on hers.

It was impossible to forget the rapture and ecstasy he had given her when he had kissed her first on the verandah and then the night when they had lain on the sofa together and she had felt as if it was impossible to go on refusing him.

"Why did I not let him do what he wanted?" she asked.

She had the feeling it was only a question of time before she would go back to him and say that she would do anything he wished as long as they could be together.

"But it would be wrong . . . wrong!" she cried out in the dark.

Yet how could anything so wonderful, so perfect, so radiant with light, be wrong?

She did not want to answer that question, but tossed and turned in her bed, telling herself that unless she went to sleep she would never be able to do all the work Mr. Garson expected of her tomorrow.

Then she heard Columbus growling.

It was the low growl he made when he was angry, and as he was normally such a very quiet dog she thought it strange.

Then as the growling continued she lit a candle, got out of bed and crossed the room to where there was a communicating door into the smaller room which adjoined hers where Danny was sleeping.

She opened the door very quietly but as she did so Columbus rushed out almost knocking her down, to stand at the other door in her bedroom which led into the outside passage.

Now he was growling again deep in his throat and had

even begun to scratch with his front paws as if he would make a hole in the floor.

"What is it, Columbus?" Roberta asked.

She spoke in a low voice so as not to disturb Danny.

Then she thought the dog must want to go out, though it was not his usual way of asking.

She picked up a light lawn wrap that lay over a chair and put it over her nightgown, then opened the door in order to take Columbus out into the garden.

There was no need for her to carry a light, for on Mr. Garson's instructions there were always one or two gas-lamps left burning in the passages.

This was so that the Night-watchman who patrolled the house every hour could see without having to carry a lantern with him.

Actually the Night-watchman, whose name was Sam, was very old, and Roberta had the suspicion that he often fell asleep in the comfortable chair that was provided for him in the hall and omitted to make his rounds.

Because everybody liked old Sam nobody would give him away to Mr. Garson.

Before his master went to bed, and again first thing in the morning, he was always to be seen looking alert and moving punctiliously round the house, inspecting the locks on the windows and on the doors.

Columbus, instead of waiting for her as Roberta had expected him to do, rushed away down the passage which led to the centre of the house and to Mr. Garson's Study.

"Columbus!" Roberta called in a low voice, but he paid no attention.

There was nothing else she could do but hurry after him, fearing that if he woke or disturbed Mr. Garson he would be very angry.

Then as she called him again he stopped and came back to her and she caught hold of his collar saying:

"What are you doing?"

To her surprise he was still growling in his throat and now a sudden thought struck her.

Suppose Columbus was actually aware of intruders in the house?

If there were, she was sure this was the way he would behave—but she was still nervous that he was just being a nuisance.

She therefore put her hand over his nose as she had seen Danny do when he was hiding him in Blue River, and said:

"Quiet, Columbus! Be quiet!"

The dog seemed to understand and crouched down as he had done when he had crept beneath the bushes to hide from the Minister.

At the same time, he pulled her forward and she realised it was in the direction of Mr. Garson's Study.

Then just before they reached it she saw a light under the door and knew that Columbus was right—there was somebody there!

She stood still and listened, and although they were very faint, she could hear movements inside.

Because the light flickered beneath the door she knew the intruder had not lit the gas-lamps as Mr. Garson would have done if he had come to his Study in the night.

Roberta then knew she must warn Sam, and pulling a reluctant Columbus with her she started to run along the passage which led to the hall.

It was a long one and so dark except for one gas-lamp at the far end of it that suddenly, when she least expected it she bumped into somebody, and realised it was a man.

She gave a stifled scream of terror.

Then she realised that instead of growling, or even barking at the man, Columbus was jumping up and down in wild excitement.

Then she felt the man's arms tighten around her and heard his voice say:

"My darling, my sweet, what are you doing here?"

She thought she must be dreaming and it could not be true, but it was Adam who spoke, Adam who was holding her, and Columbus had recognised him.

Then as she felt as if her whole world was lit with a thousand stars, she remembered Adam saying:

"I will lie, cheat, steal and even risk my life to go on painting!"

She knew then why he was there, and in a voice that was vibrant with horror, she said:

"No! No! Adam! You cannot do this! It is . . . dangerous and you will be . . . caught! I know the man you are helping is . . . inside the room, and I must tell Sam to sound the alarm!"

For a moment Adam's arms seemed to slacken a little as if he could hardly believe what he was hearing, and he wanted to look at her.

She spread out her hand on his chest and said:

"Go away . . . please go away! You cannot take them, and I have to . . . warn everybody."

"Warn everybody about what?" Adam asked.

"You know what I am talking about!"

"I have not the slightest idea," he replied. "I only know that I have found you. How could you have left me? How could you do anything so utterly damnable as to sneak away and not tell me where I could find you?"

He would have pulled her close against him again, but Roberta tried to resist him.

"Are you telling me that you are not here to . . . steal the . . . plans of the . . . engine?" she asked.

"Of course not!" he replied. "I am not interested in any damned engine, only in you!"

"Then there is a burglar in the Study!" she said. "Oh, Adam, you must help me to prevent him stealing the plans. It would break Mr. Garson's heart, and Danny's!"

Adam took his arms from her.

"Go and alert Sam," he said, "and leave this to me!"

"It may be dangerous..." Roberta started to say, but he had already moved away from her, hurrying towards the Study.

As if she felt she must obey him she ran as swiftly as she could to the end of the passage.

As she reached the hall she saw Sam coming down from the first floor, which he must have been inspecting while the burglar had got in on the ground floor.

She rushed towards him.

Only as she did so did she realise that Columbus had not followed her but had gone with Adam.

Breathless from the speed at which she had run she gasped at Sam:

"Quick... quick... sound the alarm! There is a... burglar in Mr. Garson's Study... stealing the plans of the... engine!"

Sam looked at her as if he could hardly believe what he had heard.

Then as if he was suddenly aware of what he must do he hurried across the hall to where on the wall was a siren which was worked by hand.

He started to turn it and a strange, eerie scream came from it which was echoed by amplifiers on the other floors and in the kitchens on the north side of the building.

Roberta did not wait but began to run back the way she had come.

Now she was desperately afraid that Adam, having tackled the burglar single-handed, might have been injured.

170

Burglars she knew carried pistols, and to go for one empty-handed was, she thought, a risk which only somebody like Adam would be courageous enough to attempt.

"Oh, God, do not let him be hurt... please God!" she prayed.

Then as she reached the Study she saw the door was open and Mr. Garson in his dressing-gown was entering in just ahead of her.

Even as he did so a small figure came rushing down the passage which led to their bedrooms.

She reached out to catch hold of Danny but he eluded her and slipped into the Study before she could prevent it.

"What's happening? Is there a burglar?" she heard him ask.

Then as she went through the door after him, because she was so frightened for Adam, she felt as if everything was swimming in front of her eyes, and for a moment it was impossible to see anything.

Then lying on the floor in front of the large safe which the burglar must have opened, was the body of a man, and Adam was kneeling beside him, tying up his legs with a rope from the curtains.

Columbus growling ferociously in his throat, was standing over the man who had obviously been knocked unconscious as his eyes were closed.

The handkerchief he had used to cover his face had been pulled away and Roberta could see he was a big, swarthy man with rough features and she thought he must be very strong.

It hardly seemed possible that Adam had somehow disarmed him but there was a revolver lying on the floor which must have fallen from the man's hand before he could fire it.

For a moment it was just a picture in front of her eyes

and apart from the siren still wailing in the distance there was silence until Danny cried:

"He was stealing the plans and Uncle Adam stopped him!"

Then as Adam looked round to smile at the small boy he started to say:

"Yes, I have stopped him . . ."

Then he saw who was standing beside Danny.

Adam looked at Mr. Garson and having finished knotting the rope round the unconscious burglar, he rose to his feet.

Still speaking to Danny he said:

"Columbus was there first, and he went for his throat!"

"That was very brave of Columbus."

When he had entered the room Danny had slipped his hand into Mr. Garson's and now pulling at it to attract his attention he said:

"Columbus helped to save the plans! I told you he was a good guard-dog!"

Mr. Garson did not speak.

But Roberta thought his fingers tightened over the boy's as he stood looking at Adam. Then he asked in what she thought was rather a strange voice:

"What are you doing here?"

"I have come back, Father," Adam replied. "I have decided after all, to accept your offer to work on the Railroad."

"Why?"

The monosyllable somehow seemed to ring out.

To Roberta's surprise Adam walked towards her and put his arm around her shoulders.

"This is the answer to that question," he said. "I can just keep myself as an artist, as I told you I could, but I cannot keep a wife. So I am back to where I started. I am now willing to accept your offer of a partnership."

Roberta could hardly believe what she was hearing.

Then Adam was looking down into her eyes, his arm had tightened around her, and she felt as if the moonlight was seeping through her as it had the first time he had kissed her, and the stars were enveloping them both.

For the moment they had both forgotten there was anybody else in the room, until Mr. Garson said shortly:

"I am afraid, Adam, you are too late!"

The way he spoke made Adam turn his head towards him.

"Too late, Father? But why?"

"I have filled your place," Mr. Garson said, "and my new partner is more interested in engines than you have ever been."

For a moment Roberta felt that Adam had been turned to stone. Then Mr. Garson said with a faint twist to his lips:

"I had intended if you ever came back, to introduce you to Danny, but it appears you know him already!"

It was now Adam's turn to laugh and he said:

"I do not believe it! I just do not believe it! It cannot be true!"

"It is true," Mr. Garson replied. "I may have to wait for him to grow a little bigger, but he is just the type of intelligent young man I want to work with and who really cares whether the wheels go round fast or slow, which you never did."

Adam was still laughing, but there was also a somewhat apprehensive look in his eyes.

Then Mr. Garson continued:

"And if you are intending to take Roberta away from me, it is something I shall oppose with every means in my power!"

"I am going to marry her," Adam said quietly.

"In which case, as I find her indispensable, you will have to do your painting here! After all, there is enough room."

"Do you mean that, Father? Do you really mean it?"

"I have no intention of losing you again."

Then in a soft voice that Roberta had never heard him use before he added:

"I missed you, Son."

Still with his arm around Roberta, Adam took a step forward and held out his hand to his father.

In order to shake it Mr. Garson released Danny who ran across the room to Columbus.

Roberta however had eyes only for Adam.

She heard him say in a tone which she knew was both grateful and relieved:

"Thank you, Father, and I am glad to be back."

For one second Roberta thought there was a strange moisture in Mr. Garson's eyes. Then as if he was ashamed of being sentimental he dropped Adam's hand and said sharply:

"Where the devil is everybody? That siren is making enough noise to wake the dead!"

In fact, the whole household was there, but as Mr. Garson had been standing just inside the door blocking the entrance they had not been able to pass through it.

Now they came trooping in, the men-servants picking up the burglar and carrying him away while Danny was asking anxiously if the plans were still inside the safe.

As Mr. Garson looked in it to reassure him, Adam pulled Roberta across the room to the window out of the way of everybody else.

He drew back the curtains and outside she could see that the stars were just beginning to fade from the sky and there was the first golden glow of dawn.

"Have you missed me?"

He spoke in a very low voice but she heard him.

"Terribly!"

"I was nearly off my head, frantic, searching everywhere

to find out where you could have gone."

"I thought I was . . . doing the . . . best thing for . . . you."

"I suppose it has worked out for the best because I learnt that I could not live without you, and I was prepared to give up painting so that we could be married and be together."

"I would never have allowed you to do that!"

"You would not have been able to stop me!"

He looked down at her and she thought the expression in his eyes was the most moving thing she had ever seen.

"Nothing is important except you," he said, "and I think, my darling, that is what love means."

"You . . . really . . . love me?"

It was impossible to prevent the tears from running down her cheeks because she was so happy.

Adam wiped them away and as he did so, she realised that everybody had left the Study except for Mr. Garson and Danny who were still searching in the safe to make quite certain nothing was missing.

"I love you!" Adam said, "and it is going to take a lifetime to tell you how much!"

"Did your father really mean you could go on with your painting here?"

"He said he had no intention of losing you."

"I am glad, but you know the only thing that matters is you!"

There was no need for words. Adam pulled her closer to him and she felt as if she had come home. She was his, as he was hers, and there was no need for words.

Mr. Garson rose to his feet to say:

"This safe is obviously useless! Tomorrow I will order one that no burglar will be able to open without dynamite!"

"If Uncle Adam hadn't prevented him, he might have got away with the plans!" Danny said.

"It is something which must not happen again. You and I will see to that!"

"Yes, we must see to that," Danny said in a serious little voice.

Roberta smiled at them and Mr. Garson said to her:

"Do you really intend to marry my son?"

Roberta gave a little laugh.

"He said he could not marry me because he had dedicated his life to painting, but he has changed his mind."

"I should have thought that perhaps Lady Roberta Worth was too grand to tie herself up with an impecunious Impressionist!"

"How did you find out who I am?" Roberta asked in surprise.

"My Bank Manager told me," Mr. Garson answered. "He is very impressed at having such a distinguished new client!"

Roberta laughed. Then she realised that Adam was looking at her in astonishment.

"Are you telling me that you are not Mrs. Boscombe?" he asked.

Then as she blushed, looked embarrassed, and held up her hand, he could see that there was no wedding-ring on her finger.

"I was so afraid that somebody might take Danny away from me," she explained, "that I... pretended to be his... mother."

Adam stared at her.

"How old are you?"

"I am nineteen."

"I knew it!" he exclaimed. "And how many more lies did you tell me?"

Roberta looked nervously at Mr. Garson.

"That was all," she replied. "It was simply that I was

terrified that Danny, who had been adopted by my aunt before she died, would be taken away from me and put in an Orphanage."

The word frightened Danny who jumped up from the floor.

"Now they know about me, I won't have to go into an Orphanage, will I, Aunt Roberta?" he pleaded.

There was no doubt the idea terrified him and Mr. Garson said quickly:

"If there is any trouble of that sort, I will adopt you myself."

"I think that is a very good idea, Father," Adam said. "I am sure that Danny will make up for all my deficiencies and certainly will drive an engine far better than I should ever be able to do."

Danny caught hold of Mr. Garson's hand.

"If you adopt me," he said, "you'll be my Daddy and I would like that. I love you, I love Uncle Adam, and I love Aunt Roberta very much! That would make us all a family, wouldn't it?"

Roberta knew it was what that which was in his heart, although he had never said so.

It was what he must have always wanted: to be part of a family, to be safe and free from the fear of being sent away to some strange place that was called an 'Orphanage,' or left alone and unwanted.

"You are quite right," Mr. Garson answered. "We will be a family, and doubtless in the future, you will be able to help me look after my grandchildren!"

There was a smile on his lips as he spoke, and as he looked at Roberta she blushed and pressed her cheek against Adam's shoulders.

"What we are going to do now," Mr. Garson said briskly, "is to celebrate. My son has come home, the plans have been saved and personally I not only need a strong drink, but also something to eat. Danny and I will go to tell the servants to bring what we want into the Dining-Room."

He walked away with Danny holding onto his hand.

Then Roberta thought he deliberately closed the door, shutting them both in alone.

Adam put his arms around her. Then he said:

"Lady Roberta Worth, will you do me the honour of becoming my wife?"

"I was so afraid you would never ask me!" Roberta said in a voice that was meant to be filled with laughter but was somehow a sob.

"Darling, how could you have thought for one moment that having found you I could ever lose you again?"

He kissed her hair before he said:

"And how could you have deceived me as you did, by pretending to be a married woman, although I knew when I kissed you how young, inexperienced and innocent you were?"

He turned her face up to his as he asked fiercely:

"It is true, is it not? There has never been another man in your life?"

"Of course there has not!" Roberta whispered. "Oh, Adam, I love you so much. Can we really be . . . married?"

"We will be married tonight, or rather this morning," Adam replied. "I am not waiting, and to punish you for running away from me we are not going to have a grand wedding."

"As if I would want anything so stupid!" Roberta answered.

The tears were running down her face, tears of joy because now she was with Adam again.

The agony was over, and the whole world seemed to be filled with light that he painted in his pictures.

Then she said:

"You know nothing about me. I have so much to tell you."

"I know you love me," Adam replied, "that is the only thing that matters."

Roberta gave a little sob and pressed herself against him.

"Suppose," she said in a very low voice, "I had not come to America? My father suggested it when he was dying . . . but I might have gone back to England."

Adam held her so tightly it was hard to breathe.

"Thank God you did as he suggested, my precious! If you had not obeyed him and come West I should have been lonely all my life because I had not found you."

Roberta tried to laugh.

"You might have been quite happy just with painting. But I am here, and I love you."

"And I love and worship you."

She knew from the way he spoke that it was a vow.

Then he was kissing her, kissing her wildly, possessively passionately, but at the same time with a tenderness as if she was so infinitely precious that he was half-afraid of hurting her, and still afraid of losing her.

He kissed her until once again they were moving amongst the stars and their feet were no longer on the ground.

He kissed her wet eyes, the tears from her cheeks, and again her lips.

"My precious, my lovely one!" he said. "I will never be able to tell you what an agony it was to think I had lost you! I have been walking the streets of San Francisco for the last four days, hoping that by some miracle I would see you in the crowd, and asking at every Lodging-House and Hotel if they had given accommodation to a beautiful young woman with a little boy."

He gave a laugh which still held a note of pain in it, as

if the agonies he had suffered were still very vivid.

"I was late tonight by the time I had called at about twenty lodging houses. How could I have imagined when I came home to sleep, that I would find you here, in my father's house?"

"Why did you not tell me that your father was such an important, rich man?"

"We quarrelled violently because he wanted me to work with him on the Railroad, and in particular on his plans for the fastest train in the world. He could not understand that I had to paint, that nothing else interested me. I told him I would keep myself without any help from him."

"I know now that the reason he was so kind to Danny was that he was missing you."

"Just as I missed him," Adam said. "I think, my precious one, it must have been you who softened him and made him so much more amenable and understanding than he has ever been before."

"Not me, but Danny!" Roberta corrected. "A little boy who thinks him wonderful and who is as obsessed as he is with the idea of the fastest train in the world!"

Adam laughed.

"He will be able to help my father, and I will build myself the finest Studio here that any artist ever had, and when we want to be alone, which will be very often, we will go back to the sea."

"I would like that," Roberta said. "I was happier with you there than I have ever been in my life."

"We will be there together," Adam said, "and there will be no more lonely nights for me, or for you, my darling."

Roberta gave a little murmur of happiness and he said:

"And I shall enjoy teaching our children to swim."

He spoke deliberately to see the colour come into her face. Then he laughed.

"A young girl of nineteen!" he exclaimed. "How could I have been so blind, so foolish as to believe your story that you were married?"

His lips were very near to hers as he said:

"By the time this day ends there will be no need for you to pretend to be a married woman, my precious, you will be one!"

As Roberta hid her blushes against his shoulder he went on:

"There is so much I want to teach you, so much love I have to give you, and I believe that together, my beautiful wife to be, we will find the light that I have been struggling to capture on canvas."

"The light of love," Roberta whispered, "and love is happiness. How could anything be more wonderful? Oh, Adam, we are so lucky!"

"I adore you!"

Then he was kissing her again and the light of the rising sun came through the window to touch them with gold, and the light within them made them one person for all eternity.

ABOUT THE AUTHOR

Barbara Cartland, the world's most famous romantic novelist, who is also an historian, playwright, lecturer, political speaker and television personality, has now written over 370 books and sold over 370 million books over the world.

She has also had many historical works published and has written four autobiographies as well as the biographies of her mother and that of her brother, Ronald Cartland, who was the first Member of Parliament to be killed in the last war. This book has a preface by Sir Winston Churchill and has just been republished with an introduction by Sir Arthur Bryant.

Love at the Helm, a novel written with the help and inspiration of the late Admiral of the Fleet, the Earl Mountbatten of Burma, is being sold for the Mountbatten Memorial Trust.

Miss Cartland in 1978 sang an Album of Love Songs with the Royal Philharmonic Orchestra.

In 1976 by writing twenty-one books, she broke

the world record and has continued for the following six years with twenty-four, twenty, twenty-three, twenty-four, twenty-four, and twenty-five. She is in the *Guinness Book of Records* as the best-selling author in the world.

She is unique in that she was one and two in the Dalton List of Best Sellers, and one week had four books in the top twenty.

In private life Barbara Cartland, who is a Dame of the Order of St. John of Jerusalem, Chairman of the St. John Council in Hertfordshire and Deputy President of the St. John Ambulance Brigade, has also fought for better conditions and salaries for Midwives and Nurses.

Barbara Cartland is deeply interested in Vitamin Therapy and is President of the British National Association for Health. Her book *The Magic of Honey* has sold throughout the world and is translated into many languages. Her designs "Decorating with Love" are being sold all over the USA, and the National Home Fashions League made her in 1981, "Woman of Achievement."

Barbara Cartland's Romances (a book of cartoons) has recently been published in Great Britain and the U.S.A., as well as a cookery book, *The Romance of Food*.